A PRINCE OF MY OWN

Forever Yours Series

STACY REID

A PRINCE OF MY OWN is a work of fiction. While reference might be made to actual historical events or existing locations, the names, characters, places, and incidents are either the product of the author's imagination or are used fictitiously, and any resemblance to actual persons, living or dead, business establishments, events, or locales are entirely coincidental.

All rights reserved. No part of this book may be reproduced in any form by any electronic or mechanical means—except in the case of brief quotations embodied in critical articles or reviews—without written permission.

First Edition April 2019

Edited by AuthorsDesigns
Copy-edited by Gina Fiserova
Proofread by Monique Daoust
Cover design and formatting by AuthorsDesigns
Stock art from Period Images
Copyright © 2019 by Stacy Reid

Dusean, always and forever.

FREE OFFER

SIGN UP TO MY NEWSLETTER TO CLAIM YOUR FREE BOOK!

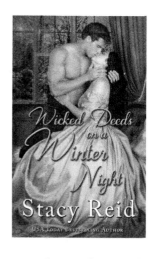

To claim your FREE copy of Wicked Deeds on a Winter Night, a delightful and sensual romp to indulge in your reading addiction, please click here.

Once you've signed up, you'll be among the first to hear about my new releases, read excerpts you won't find anywhere else, and patriciate in subscriber's only giveaways and contest. I send out on dits once a month and on super special occasion I might send twice, and please know you can unsubscribe whenever we no longer zing.

Happy reading!
Stacy Reid

PRAISE FOR NOVELS OF
STACY REID

"**Duchess by Day, Mistress by Night** is a sensual romance with explosive chemistry between this hero and heroine!"—*Fresh Fiction Review*

"From the first page, Stacy Reid will captivate you! Smart, sensual, and stunning, you will not want to miss **Duchess by Day, Mistress by Night**!"—*USA Today bestselling author Christi Caldwell*

"I would recommend **The Duke's Shotgun Wedding** to anyone who enjoys passionate, fast-paced historical romance."—*Night Owl Reviews*

"**Accidentally Compromising the Duke**—Ms. Reid's story of loss, love, laughter and healing is all that I look for when reading romance and deserving of a 5-star review." —*Isha C., Hopeless Romantic*

"Wicked in His Arms—Once again Stacy Reid has left me spellbound by her beautifully spun story of romance between two wildly different people." —*Meghan L., LadywithaQuill.com*

"Wicked in His Arms—I truly adored this story and while it's very hard to quantify, this book has the hallmarks of the great historical romance novels I have read!" —*KiltsandSwords.com*

"One for the ladies...**Sins of a Duke** is nothing short of a romance lover's blessing!" —*WTF Are You Reading*

"THE ROYAL CONQUEST is raw, gritty and powerful, and yet, quite unexpectedly, it is also charming and endearing." —*The Romance Reviews*

OTHER BOOKS BY STACY

Series Boxsets

Forever Yours Series Bundle (Book 1-3)

Forever Yours Series Bundle (Book 4-6)

Forever Yours Series Bundle (Book 7-9)

The Amagarians: Book 1-3

Sinful Wallflowers series

My Darling Duke

Her Wicked Marquess

Forever Yours series

The Marquess and I

The Duke and I

The Viscount and I

Misadventures with the Duke

When the Earl was Wicked

A Prince of my Own

Sophia and the Duke

The Sins of Viscount Worsley

An Unconventional Affair

Mischief and Mistletoe

A Rogue in the Making

The Kincaids

Taming Elijah

Tempting Bethany

Lawless: Noah Kincaid

Rebellious Desires series

Duchess by Day, Mistress by Night

The Earl in my Bed

Wedded by Scandal Series

Accidentally Compromising the Duke

Wicked in His Arms

How to Marry a Marquess

When the Earl Met His Match

Scandalous House of Calydon Series

The Duke's Shotgun Wedding

The Irresistible Miss Peppiwell

Sins of a Duke

The Royal Conquest

The Amagarians

Eternal Darkness

Eternal Flames

Eternal Damnation

Eternal Phoenyx

Single Titles

Letters to Emily

Wicked Deeds on a Winter Night

The Scandalous Diary of Lily Layton

CHAPTER 1

Lady Miranda Elizabeth Cheswick's first memories were of her mother extolling her great beauty, and that she would one day marry a prince, or most certainly a duke. As the daughter of one of the most renowned and influential earls in the realm, it was expected any match she made was to a man of rank, respectability, and great fortune. To that end, her mother, the Countess of Langford, had made it her duty since Miranda's come out three years ago to hunt a gentleman who fit those standards of the Cheswick family, with a single-minded intensity that Miranda admitted could be frightening and at times embarrassing.

Of course, her mamma did not regard her matrimonial fervor in the same light. The countess had often said Miranda's incomparable beauty, grace, charm, and wit could not be wasted on a gentleman of mediocrity, and over the years the countess had impressed upon her daughter that very belief. And for so long Miranda had faithfully believed her beauty should only allow for the best in her life, and that belief had cost her the dearest of friendships. A friendship which Miranda had treasured. The rift between her and Pippa, the new Duchess of Carlyle, was so terrible they had not spoken in almost two months. And there was nothing Miranda wanted more than to mend that relationship.

She slowly lowered the newssheet which mentioned the Duke and Duchess of Carlyle were back in town after several weeks of traveling. A visit must be paid at once, and despite the fearful ache in her heart and the doubt rising inside, there must be no delay.

The door to the drawing room swung open then slammed shut as her mother marched inside in a swirling green dress and swishing petticoat. Miranda had been waiting for over two hours for this confrontation, for nothing had gone how her mother had planned it last night. She braced for the severe scolding that was about to be delivered.

"You will not disappoint our expectations ever again, young lady," her mamma cried without any preamble, her violet eyes brimming with tears and unjust reproach. "It is your duty to this family to marry and marry well! I'll not hear any more objections, Miranda!"

Miranda sat on the chaise longue, her spine rigid yet elegantly poised, daring not to blink as her mother scolded her most ferociously for yet another failure in snagging the man everyone had said was the catch of the season. "Mamma, I can explain—"

"Three eminently suitable suitors you have lost now! *Three*. You encouraged the Grand Prince Vladimir Konstantinovich to turn his regard to Miss Harriet Shelby, and now they are engaged! Why I still cannot credit it, a Russian prince with that nobody! Then the Duke of Carlyle was ripe for your plucking. I did everything to ensure you ensnared him and somehow, you foolish girl, you allowed him to get away. And I had the Marquess of Blythe conveniently locked in the conservatory with you at last night's soirée! I had to pay a servant to discreetly deliver a note to you and the marquess, and you…you had the nerve to slip through a window to escape!"

Papa had often remarked fondly of the devious

ways mamma had secured his hand for marriage more than twenty-five years past. It seemed her mother required her to act similarly and did not hide that it was her expectations. She lifted her chin, hating to recall the shock of horror she'd felt last night when she realized what her mother had planned. "Mamma, Lord Blythe inspires little emotion in my heart."

Though the marquess was declared as handsome and a man of fashion and elegance, whenever he touched her, she felt cold and unmoved. Miranda had begun to wonder if passion truly existed. "He has never asked me about what I like to do or how I spend my day. He only compliments my beauty and—"

The countess shook her head as if in a daze. "You ungrateful, wretched girl! We have worked so hard to cultivate your reputation as a diamond of the *ton*, and you speak as if you wish it were not so!"

Over the last few years, Miranda had become a well sought-after social butterfly, coveted by the young bucks of each season. During the social season, her days were spent assisting her mother in ordering the household, planning balls, musicales, routs, and picnics. She was admired often by both ladies and gents for her exquisite grace and form when dancing, and her skill at the pianoforte. It was often remarked that she would make a fine wife with her excellent upbringing, amiable disposition, and breathtaking beauty.

"An engagement should have been in the papers today!"

Her mother's cries were like a stone scraping against glass.

"Mamma," she said, standing, her heart pounding with discomfort for she had never been one to contradict her mother. But the situation had becoming intolerable, the season no longer fun and intriguing. Until recent events, Miranda anticipated each season with elation for all the thrilling events she would attend and the courtship dances. She had been enthralled by the excitement of attending lavish balls, picnics, carriage rides, and walking out and flirting with several suitors. Now, only dread knotted her stomach whenever she thought about the next season and the marriage mart. "If I am such a sorry disappointment it is little wonder you do not banish me from your sight to the country with grandmamma."

That would be far more tolerable than the constant pressure from her mamma to secure any eligible gentleman that came on the market. The tedium of country life was vastly more appealing than the parties of the little season. In Lincolnshire, she could take long walks, visit the orphanage her grandmamma sponsored, and perhaps attend a few balls at the local assembly. But most importantly, there she would have space and the freedom to think about what she wanted from life, and not what her mother insisted she must possess.

"This season you have put my nerves out of sort most abominably, and you danced with Mr. Brandon last night! Why would you do something so foolish?"

With a sigh, she pushed a few loose wisps of hair behind her ears. "He is very good-natured and charming mamma, and he is the younger brother of a viscount, so he is not without connections." And he had appeared so earnest and anxious when he asked, she'd not the heart to reject him, and she'd had a wonderful time dancing the quadrille and the polka with Mr. Brandon.

The countess advanced further into the drawing room, the glint in her eyes a dangerous thing to behold. "You will politely decline his offer if he should approach you again. He is not the sort of man a young lady of your connections and propriety should extend the smallest encouragement even if it is only dancing!"

Her whole life it had been impressed upon her the type of man she was to marry. A prince. A duke. Her mother would possibly accept a marquess if he possessed considerable estates and wealth. There had never been a mention of the man's character, and it saddened her to realize it honestly did not matter to her mother or to most society members. Invariably she shared a similar truth. The men who pursued her had no liking for her mind nor were they curious about learning about her. Her beauty, connections, and dowry were all that was admired.

Her mother sniffed as if holding back tears. "The entire day I've despaired with your father about what we should do with you. Miranda, you are two and twenty. You should be running and organizing your own household. Why, at eighteen I was already with child with your brother."

"Mamma please, might we enjoy the rest of our stay in town without conversations about whom I'm to secure?"

Her mother stiffened as if she could not indeed countenance such a suggestion. "We planned to receive an offer this season! By next week everyone will be off to their country estates, and all opportunities will be lost until next year. Despite all my efforts in securing you a proper match you have willfully thwarted my best efforts."

Her mother's best efforts referred to the Duke of Carlyle, a man who had gone on to marry Miranda's friend, Pippa, in a rare and beautiful love match of the season a few months ago. Her mother's wicked wiles and Miranda's foolish heart had allowed her to go along with her mother's disastrous plan to compromise the Duke of Carlyle. Mamma had been determined for him to be her son-in-law, and Miranda had been committed to becoming a duchess. She had snuck into the man's room at a house party a few months ago, with the sole intention of compromising his honor so he would be forced to marry her.

The very memory of that scene had humiliation and shame crawling through her veins. She felt as if she aged several years since. Once she had taken it as her due that a man would look upon her face and fall hopelessly in love. That with a smile she would be able to ensnare him. She had rested much upon her beauty and had ignored her honor and common sense to her undying shame. "I do not wish to attend Lady Peregrine's house party,

Mamma. Might I travel down to grandmother instead?"

Her mother's eyes narrowed. "That is our last event before we retire to the country with your father. I have it on good authority Lord Blythe will be in attendance, and I expect, young lady, an offer from him by the end of the party."

"And am I to secure that offer by any means?" she demanded scathingly with pain and anger beating in her heart. "Did you know I was silly and willful enough to try to compromise the Duke of Carlyle a few months ago, doing exactly as you suggested, Mamma? I slipped into his room at Lady Burrell's garden party! And Mamma…I went only in my banyan."

Shock glazed her mother's eyes, and she moved forward with jerky steps. "And he did not offer for you? How outrageous and dishonorable of him!"

Miranda rubbed her temples, hoping to soothe the headache she could feel forming. "Mamma, it was *my* conduct which was outrageous. He should have thrown me out on my head! Instead, he did the gentlemanly thing by walking away. And I was so humiliated at my failure I did not tell my dear friend the truth, and she then waged a campaign to destroy the duke's reputation when it had been unwarranted. Since then my eyes have been opened, the shame in my heart laid bare, and the regret in my heart heavy."

Her mother stared at her for several seconds. "You are simply too harsh with yourself, my dear. It was my expectation that you would secure the duke this season. It is a disappointment we must all bear, and it does us no credit to speak about what happened at that garden party. We shall rally and prepare for next season the best we can. I do have high hopes regarding Lord Blythe. While not the title we had hoped for you, the marquess has considerable estate and wealth. Now hurry to your rooms and ensure all is well for our journey in the morning."

A girl of your astonishing beauty must only marry a prince…or a duke…, I declare to be so! Refrains she had heard from when she was a twelve year-old child in the schoolroom. Words which had made her once preen, her chest puffed with pride, now made her feel sick to her stomach, and her throat aching with unshed tears. "If you'll excuse me, Mamma."

She left the drawing room and her mother, but instead of heading upstairs, she collected her pelisse and bonnet having already called for the carriage. Almost thirty minutes later, she made her way to the townhouse of the Duke and Duchess of Carlyle in Portman Square.

Miranda bravely knocked on the large oak door, and when the butler made his appearance, she asked to see the duke and duchess. He allowed her inside and led her to the drawing room where a merry fire crackled in the hearth. She tried to marshal her thoughts, unsure of what she would say to Pippa and to the duke. The words eluded her, and the only guidance she had was the awful ache of regret in her heart and the burn of tears lodged in her throat.

"Miranda!"

She whirled around at her name to see a glowing Pippa gliding into the room. Shock tore through Miranda when Pippa enfolded her into a warm hug. There was no help for it, a sob tore from her throat. "Oh, Pippa, I have been so wretched with shame at my conduct. I have used you ill, and I am so very sorry!"

"Hush now," Pippa said, her own voice choked with emotions. "I regret leaving on my travels without mending our fences. You had apologized to me, and I ignored your overtures. Come, let's sit and talk." Looping their arms together, the duchess led her over to the sofa closest to the fire. The warmth seeped into Miranda's bones, thawing the cold knot of doubt which had constricted her muscles.

A sound alerted, and she glanced up to see the duke. Miranda flushed, discomfort crawling through her veins. She had slipped into this man's room and had shrugged off her robe! The room had been very dark, and she had doubted he even knew it was her, but the very memory of it made her want to die of humiliation. She stood. "Your Grace, I am so very sorry."

He smiled warmly, rendering her mute. "That is in the past, Lady Miranda. If I recall, more than five months ago. I probably should not say it, but without your antics, my darling Pippa would not have turned her mischievous wiles in my direction, and I would possibly have missed my love. So, I should be thanking you, hmmm?"

A laugh hiccupped from her. "You are both very generous, and I thank you for it."

And there was an easing inside that swelled and expanded through every crevice of her being. The duke lingered for a few minutes, engaging her in discourse before he excused himself. Miranda turned to Pippa, "You do appear radiant, Pippa. I am so pleased with your happiness."

Her friend squeezed her hand. "I cannot wait for you to find similar happiness. With your great beauty and poise, any day now—"

She tugged her hand away from Pippa. "Do you also believe a man would only be interested in me because of my beauty?" she cried. "Oh, Pippa, I do not want that! I want the gentleman whom I marry to see beyond that and see me! I want this even as I wonder who I am, Pippa. But I am most certain, I want to love the man I marry and also to know beyond doubt that he loves me just as ardently. I want to share my fears and dreams, and failures as they come and know I will always find comfort in his arms. Is it silly of me to hunger for this?"

Pippa smiled gently. "Oh, Miranda, it is an inescapable fact that you are lovely. You enter a room and men stare covetously, ladies glower in envy, many mothers worry you will outshine their daughters. Each season you receive numerous offers which your mother rejects. It is inevitable a man will see your beauty first, but I daresay if he is worth his salt, he will hunger to know the passionate heart that beats within you. And if he is fortunate for you to return his regard, he will then discover how kind and caring you are. How filled with good fun and humor, how passionate you are about art and music and I daresay he will love you."

She hugged her friend tightly. "Thank you, Pippa, I needed to hear this."

"I missed you," Pippa said softly, returning her fierce embrace. "I miss our long walks and talks. Let's promise nothing should ever come between us again."

"I promise it," Miranda said.

Almost an hour later she made her way home, a new purpose growing in unchecked leaps and bounds in her heart. From the age of twelve, she had been relentlessly groomed on how to become a wife, how to organize and run a household, and how to select charitable organizations to sponsor. Most attachments she'd observed throughout the seasons appeared cold and impersonal, with both ladies and their lords seeking other lovers to soothe the heartache of loneliness. She couldn't endure such a union. The notion of marrying a gentleman for his monetary worth and title, without possessing an ounce of regard for the man no longer sat well with her.

Miranda hungered to find her own place within the world which did not solely follow her mamma's guidance. She did want a prince of her own, a gentleman who would love her as she would love him, a gentleman with whom she could build a happy life and home. But for the first time since Miranda's come out four years ago, she secretly pledged to only marry a man she loved and one who possessed similar sentiments.

The Marquess of Blythe was the next man her mother had deemed a perfect match for her daughter. Such was his consequences that he could pick any of the debutantes of the season and they would fall gratefully at his feet. It was generally thought his age of five and fifty could be overlooked for his vast fortune and immeasurable connection. Indeed, her mother expected her to overlook the matter, and completely ignore that she would want to marry for a more tender sentiment.

This time she was determined to be the one to choose the man she wished to walk with, to dance with at balls, and to admire. *Don't worry, Mamma, I will ensure he is a prince...or a duke!* And that way she would not disappoint her family's expectation of her, but she would also be true to her heart.

CHAPTER 2

Simon Percival Astor lifted the young child atop his head to her delight and started a riveting story of wicked witches, princesses, and princes as they strolled along the eastern sections of his estate. The young girl, Emma who had recently recovered from influenza, chortled and gripped tufts of his hair in her excitement.

"Oh, and what happened to the princess after she bit the apple from the wicked witch?" Emma demanded breathlessly.

Simon winced at another tug at his hair, but carried on, his four wolfhounds yipping with excitement at his heels. It had been a fight to save six year-old Emma's life, and she had been in his home and under his care for almost three weeks.

Her mother, his housekeeper, would be quite relieved at her daughter's progress. They moved at a very brisk pace, for in the distance the breeze moved the clouds swollen with rain closer to him. The deluge would arrive any minute now, and he needed to get little Emma to shelter before it came. It would not do for her to be soaked only days after leaving the sickbed.

"Hurry, Dr. Astor," the child yelled, as a fat drop of rain splattered on the ground. "The rain is coming!"

Holding firmly to her knees dangling over each of his shoulders, Simon broke into a light, careful run. The child screamed her glee, before breaking into fits of cough. He listened keenly to hear if that awful rattle lingered on her chest and was pleased it did not. They made it inside safely, and with the swift agility of a monkey she clambered down his back with his assistance.

Her mother, Mrs. Clayton, hurried down the hallway, her hands twisting in her apron. The child barreled toward her and was soon swept up into a hug.

"Doctor," Mrs. Clayton said, "Jim was calling for you. There was a carriage accident by the river, and he fears people might have been hurt, Sir!"

"Are the carriages on the bridge? Or did they make it safely over?"

The housekeeper's face creased with concern. "On it, Sir."

Biting back a curse, he ran to his study, grabbed his medical bag and hurried from the manor. The housekeeper had smartly called for his horse, and the small carriage had been readied and waiting. He vaulted onto his horse and nodded to Jim, the coachman. "Follow at a good speed, my man, I will ride ahead." Then he surged away, uncaring the skies had opened, and rain pounded down furiously.

The bridge abutted his land only three miles to the east and was known to collapse when the rivers were swollen from a deluge. It took several minutes riding at top speed along the muddied lanes before Simon reached the crash site, and a cursory glance did not show any fatalities. He sent a swift prayer for small mercies as he dismounted and hurried over. The carriages seemed to have collided trying to pass each other on the narrow bridge. He had paid for significant repairs to be done on the bridge only a few months past, and the slats and ropes seemed to be holding steady. The waters below churned violently, it was an intimidating sight to behold.

Simon hurried to a carriage where three men were busy unloading traveling bags and roping them together. He assumed the coachman and his tiger, and perhaps a footman. Clearly, this first carriage belonged to a family of wealth.

"I'm a doctor," he shouted to be heard over the pounding rain. "Where are the injured?"

The door opened, and inside the darkened carriage he made out the form of three ladies and a gentleman. They seemed more frightened than harmed. One of the ladies' back was to him as she pressed a lace handkerchief to another woman's forehead who appeared to be unconscious. He hopped into the darkened interiors of the carriage, seeing that the oil from the carriage lantern had spilled.

"Who are you?" the man clipped in tight accents, glancing up from the prostrate woman.

"I'm the doctor."

"I'm Viscount Sutton, and my mother needs immediate attention."

Simon turned to the lady in the left corner who held her arm as if pained. He deduced from her dress she was a traveling companion, a maid within their household. "Are you hurt?" he asked gently, seeing the glaze of shock in her eyes.

She shook her head and pressed a hand to her trembling lips.

The young lady of quality bent over the prostrate lady glanced up, but he was unable to discern her features.

"I fear the occupants in the other carriages may be hurt. I heard screams a few seconds ago. I tasked my brother to investigate, but he seemed to be afraid of getting his fine waistcoat wet!"

Her voice was sweet and refined, and quite annoyed.

"Good God, Mira, it is squalling outside. Surely you did not really expect me to go out in that. I also asked the coachman and his tiger to look," the viscount huffed.

She muttered something under her breath, then said with perfect clarity, "I believe Mamma has fainted. She was quite hysterical a few minutes past and then she collapsed on the cushions," she said worriedly.

Simon leaned in to check the lady's pulse. It was strong and steady. "There is no indication of serious distress," he reassured the daughter, dipping into his medical bag. He wafted an aromatic vinaigrette below the lady's nose, she twitched then groaned, but kept her eyes closed.

"My man is coming behind me with a carriage pulled by a team of four. He will escort you to my home a few miles from here. I'll arrange for your valises to be taken there as well."

"Thank you," the young lady gasped. "We are most appreciative of your kindness, Sir."

"And where is your home?" the brother asked with arrogant disdain. "I cannot imagine anything presentable or of reasonable quality in this godforsaken part of Hertfordshire. Are there no inns nearby?"

Simon ignored him, quickly dismounted, and headed over to the next carriage. He wrenched the door open and spied a wailing lady clutching a small boy in her arms. There was a deep gash on his head, and he bled profusely.

"My Tommy won't wake," she said, crying copiously.

Simon entered the carriage and took the boy from her. He appeared around eight years of age. Simon arranged him on the seat of the carriage and pressed a clean strip of linen soaked in crushed-berry vinegar to the wound. "There now, let me attend him. I'm a doctor."

The lady visibly wilted with relief. The boy's pulse was a bit weak and more erratic. Simon scrutinized the boy's head, seeking more cuts and bumps and did not find any. He dipped into his bag, retrieved more bandages, and quickly wrapped them around the open gash. "My home is a few miles away. If you will allow me to escort you there."

"Are they well?" a voice cried from behind him.

He twisted around to see the young lady from the next carriage standing in the rain. Her bonnet hung limply on her forehead hiding most of her features, and the narrow-waisted dress clung alluringly to her slim, elegant figure.

She pushed her head inside the carriage. "Is there anything I can do to assist, Sir?"

The offer surprised him so much he stared for a few seconds. "Mrs....." He turned to the still weeping woman.

"Mrs. Denniston," she hiccupped.

Simon nodded. "Mrs. Denniston could use some comfort. Her son has taken quite a knock on the head and must be attended to right away."

The clatter of his carriage sounded, and the young lady glanced around. "I believe your carriage is here, Sir!"

And so it was. The young lady stepped back, and he stepped out of the carriage. He beckoned one of the footmen over, who jumped into the carriage, lifted the boy and placed him in Simon's arm. The young lady, Mira if he recalled the name her brother used correctly, hurried over and assisted Mrs. Denniston down. A loud gasp sounded from the young lady, and he shifted his regard to them and immediately saw the cause for that breathy sound.

Mrs. Denniston's bosoms were fairly spilling out of her red dress, and upon closer inspection, he supposed she would not be the kind of woman with whom a young lady would consort. A memory teased, and he seemed to recall a rumor that Esquire Johnson had retained the widowed Mrs. Denniston as his mistress.

A swell of admiration rose for the young lady, as she gently took Mrs. Denniston's hand and led her off the bridge to the waiting carriage. Upon his approach he heard Mira gently assuring her that Tommy would be well, assurances Simon himself never gave. A head wound might very well be perilous, though he would do everything in his power to ensure the boy mend.

Mrs. Denniston was made comfortable in the

carriage, and he laid the boy on the cushions and placed his head gently in her lap. Then he dipped into his bag and waved smelling salts under his nose. The boy jerked, and that was a good enough sign for Simon.

The viscount hurried over with their mother clasped against his side, and from the look of it, she had come around. They entered the carriage, and she shuffled over to the corner, her wide violet eyes pinned on Mrs. Denniston's revealing attire.

The rain had blessedly lessened, and Simon hurriedly closed the door on the occupants—Mira, her mother and brother, Mrs. Denniston and her son Tommy.

"Take them to the manor," he said. "Send more men to attend with unhitching the horses and lead them to the stables. The village blacksmith will also need to attend to the carriages."

Everyone hurried to do his bidding, and Simon made his way over to his horse and followed.

A LARGE-BONED and quite handsome woman ushered Miranda, her brother, and Mamma inside a large and brightly lit manor house. When the carriage had drawn up in the circular driveway, the doctor had assisted Mrs. Denniston and her son toward a side entrance and disappeared with them. This lady had been awaiting them and had urged them inside before the rains returned. Inside was warm, inviting, and the scent of lemon, beeswax, and roasting meat was redolent on the air. Miranda's stomach made an embarrassing rumble, reminding her they had not eaten since breaking their fast early that morning before departing the inn.

"I'm Mrs. Clayton, and I am the housekeeper here at Riversend Manor. I'll soon show you to your rooms and supper will be ready by seven. There are blankets in the parlor with tea and cakes, if you'll follow me," she said with a kind smile.

"Who is the lord of this manor?" Miranda's mother imperiously demanded of the hovering housekeeper. "I expect the best rooms to be prepared right away." Her lips were pinched in pain and when she tried to move the countess cried out in pain.

"Mother, what is it?" Henry asked, his brows furrowed with concern.

Mamma had insisted he accompanied them to Lady Peregrine's house party, putting a halt to the amusements he had planned for himself in town. Her brother had not been a happy follower, but invariably he always obeyed Mamma's commands.

"My right ankle pains me horribly," she replied, her eyes watering.

"I'll summon Dr. Astor right away, milady," Mrs. Clayton replied and scuttled from the room.

Miranda swiped the wet ringlets from her face and glanced around. It was an impressive manor and elegantly appointed. The hallway was lined with richly carved oak paneling, and the décor one of luxurious elegance. How fortunate a physician had been on call here and could have attended them so readily. She dearly hoped that the little boy would be well.

The sound of booted feet echoed in the distance and the man who had been out in the ghastly weather barking commands appeared. In the dark by the bridge, it had been very hard to ascertain his features. Now under the warm glow of candles and lamps, he looked a bit wild and unkempt but so astonishingly virile he stole her breath.

His Hessian boots were muddied, his black hair plastered to his forehead, his white shirt clung to the wall of his chest, and with each movement, the muscles rippled and twisted. The man was shockingly without a jacket or a waistcoat, and his cravat was unknotted. His gaze narrowed in on Miranda. His eyes were the darkest blue of midnight—and she fancied she could drown in their unfathomable depths. A sweet, mystifying ache trembled low in her belly, and it appalled her for she'd never had such a reaction to any gentleman before in all her years. It shocked her that he did not give her more than a cursory glance. No doubt she looked like a drowned rat.

Those eyes returned to her. "Are you hurt, miss?"

Before she could reply, her mother bit out, "It is Lady Miranda to you, Sir, and I am Countess Langford."

Brief irritation furrowed his brow, but then he bowed with charming elegance and clipped, "Are you hurt, Lady Miranda?"

"Are you a physician?" her mother demanded.

"I am, my lady. I am Dr. Simon Astor."

Her belly flipped when his regard returned to her. "I ask again, are you hurt?"

She assessed him with a critical eye. "I am not, Sir, but Mamma has been piteously complaining of a pain in her ankle."

He moved then with sharp competency despite her mother's bluster.

"May I have permission to lift you in my arms, my lady?"

Her mother gasped, flushed, and glared at him. Miranda bit back her smile.

"If you wish, I could summon two footmen to assist you. Or perhaps your son might do the honors."

Her mother nodded, and he swept her into his arms with impressive strength. With quick strides, he made his way down the hallway, and Miranda hurried after them with Henry following. A maid opened a large oak-paneled door, and they entered a small but tastefully furnished parlor. He lowered her mother to the chaise longue with care, then glanced at the hovering maid.

"A basin of warm water, towels, and strips of linens. Also the rubbing liniment."

The maid hurried away to do his bidding. A clap of thunder startled Miranda, and she rushed to her mother's side. The doctor tried to remove her mother's boot to her great distress. Her pain was genuine, and she clasped her mother's hand and muttered soothing nonsense.

"We will have to cut this boot off," he said.

"The ankle is too swollen and will cause you considerable pain if I should attempt to tug it off."

Her mother's eyes glistened with tears, and her lips were pinched. "Very well," she said with a sniff. "Please do hurry about it, I am dreadfully uncomfortable and put out!"

A decidedly imperious brow rose from the doctor, but he made no reply and went to work, and soon after the swollen ankle was freed. The stockings were removed, and Miranda gasped to see the awful mottled purple which surrounded her mother's ankle down to her toes.

"Good heaven, mother!" Henry exclaimed, bending for a closer inspection.

"What is wrong?" Miranda asked anxiously.

Dr. Astor sent her a reassuring smile while tenderly probing her mother's ankle. "It seems there is a bad sprain."

"I believe it happened when I was flung from the seat of the carriage, and I struggled to find purchase. I placed most of my weight on this right leg, and there was horrible pain," her mother said fretfully.

"I will soak it in a bit of warm water and, my lady, you will have to be off this foot for at least a week."

"A week! Dr. Astor," her mother began, appearing considerably stricken. Henry looked as if he had been given a reprieve from the hangman's noose, and Miranda wanted to do a happy twirl.

"That just will not do. My daughter and I have a house party to attend, and it starts tomorrow. We *must* be there! Please summon the master of this residence."

"At your service, madam."

Her mother stared at him in apparent shock. It was unexpected for a physician to have such evident wealth and property. It was unusual, and Miranda stared at him with abashed inquisitiveness.

"Well," the countess said, "I would like for you to have your best carriage ready so we may depart early tomorrow."

Dr. Astor stood. "You are a great deal too injured to move. There might be a small fracture, and once the swelling reduces, I shall bind your ankle with linens. I daresay it may be a full two weeks before I would recommend any walking and another three for dancing."

He glanced outside into the sleeting rains. The doctor strode over to the window and stood looking out. After a few minutes, he said, "This weather will also not permit any traveling for a few days."

As if to support the doctor's assurances, thunder rumbled, and fat heavy drops of rain descended from the sky, slapping against the glass like pebbles. Her mother was sorely vexed by this and did not hesitate to voice her displeasure.

"I shall have the three best rooms in the manor to lay our head," she said with such arrogance Miranda winced.

She ambled forward tugging at her wet bonnet which was becoming an irritant. She untied the strings of her bonnet and removed it with a sigh of relief. Dr. Astor's sharp intake of breath was audible for all to hear and Miranda flushed, appalled at the piercing pleasure which burst inside her chest. They stared at each other, and she was painfully aware that her mother and brother glanced from the doctor to her.

His regard skipped over her face slowly, as if he memorized her features. Her skin burned pleasantly where his gaze had touched, her pulse tripped alarmingly, and a flush rose on her skin. Noting her reactions, the doctor's mouth curved in a slow, unsettling smile before his mien was rendered unreadable.

"Mamma is in pain, Dr. Astor. We shall thankfully receive whichever rooms are available."

He considered her for several moments, his expression still carefully inscrutable. "It would be my honor if you would be my guests until you are both fit to travel, Lady Langford, Lady Miranda, and Lord Sutton."

He rang the bell, and a maid appeared. The doctor was a bit curt with his instructions, and Miranda wondered at the change in his temperament. Not that he was overly pleasant before, but now he seemed downright uncivil.

"Dinner here is simple but quite appetizing. You may join me in the dining hall at seven or request a tray for your rooms. Whichever is preferred." Then he departed the parlor.

"Henry, you will go ahead with Miranda to Lady Peregrine's—"

"I'll not leave your side, Mamma," Miranda said firmly. "And you shall not be able to convince me of it. The house party is lost to us, and you must recover so we can travel to Lincolnshire to be with papa."

Her mother huffed her agreement, though her dismay was evident for all to see. Soon Miranda was comfortably fitted into an elegantly designed bedchamber. Her room was next to her mother's, a bit smaller, but just as tastefully furnished. Henry had been placed further down the hall, but from the lack of complaint from him, she gathered he was pleased with the accommodations. A bath was delivered to her delight, and she soaked away the rain, mud, and travel from the day at her leisure. She was pleasantly surprised a maid had been sent up to assist her with her toiletries. Miranda slipped into her nightgown, too weary to head downstairs for dinner. At her request, a tray was brought to her, and she quickly consumed the delicious meal of roasted beef, baked trout, asparagus, and baked sliced potatoes in crème sauce. She also drank half the content of the decanter of sherry which had accompanied the meal.

The tray was left outside her door, and she climbed into the bed with a gusty sigh. The disaster of the house party had been averted. Folding her hand beneath her cheek, she turned onto her side and attempted to drift away into slumber.

Dark blue eyes, and sharp cheekbones teased behind her eyelids. The way he had inhaled as he stared at her, yet his eyes had given nothing away. *Did you find me beautiful?* Her body trembled in reaction to the awareness she wanted him to find her attractive. Miranda felt sure she would expire from the shock.

Her eyes flew open, Miranda lurched upright in the bed and touched her cheeks and below her throat. "I am not fevered," she muttered with annoyance. "Then why am I thinking of a gentleman I've met for all of five minutes?"

It shocked her to realize she was not impervious to the doctor's charm. Any such attraction to a man her family would never consider to be a good match would surely be perilous and silly, yet she could not deny what she had felt. Perhaps that ache in her heart and fluttery feeling low in her stomach had been an aberration, and in the morning when she saw the doctor, her pulse would not tremble at all. For all she knew the man could be odious in his character, an ogre with no redeeming qualities. She closed her eyes, recalling the tender and kind way he had assisted Mrs. Denniston and her son, the way he had treated Mamma despite her arrogance and sense of superiority. No, the doctor was a kind man…and perhaps with many more layers to his character. Miranda drifted to sleep wishing she would eventually know all of them.

CHAPTER 3

The doctor's manor was a lovely, spacious, sixty-room building which sat on several acres of land with the most beautiful lake set in the grounds of the property. Based on Miranda's cursory inspection after breaking her fast, the ballroom which folded into the large drawing room had been converted to a hospital of a sort, with several small beds, and sofas with many cushions in the rooms for patients. She had peeked around the door, and had seen the young lad, Tommy, resting with four other children, three girls and a small boy, each slumbering on separate beds. Miranda had slipped away, astonished at the doctor's generosity.

Her mother had hobbled from her room with Henry's help, despite the doctor's order that she should remain off her feet. Mamma had regretted it and had managed to hurt herself more. Dr. Astor had once more soaked her foot in warm water and had gently rubbed a pungent-smelling ointment on her mother's extremities. Then he had lifted her in his arms, mounted the stairs with such ease, and deposited the countess to her room. It had amused Miranda to notice her mother blushing and staring at the muscles of the doctor's arms.

The sky remained overcast, so any long walk would not be wise, and Miranda found herself out of sorts and perplexed with what to do with her time. She had spent an hour touring the grounds of the estate before the threatening rains had forced her indoors. Slipping into the room the housekeeper indicated was the library, she faltered on the threshold, gasping with surprised pleasure. His library was wonderful! Elegantly shelved walls of books rose in splendor. The library was decorated in antique red, blue, and gold, with four soaring windows facing the rolling expanse of the estate grounds. Mahogany bookcases lined the walls and rose beyond the second floor extending to the vaulted ceiling. There was even a ladder to climb for fetching and returning books, and there was a staircase for the higher levels. Her feet sank into plush Aubusson carpet as she glided across the expanse of the room, truly struck by the beauty of the library. It was at least three times the size of the libraries in each of her homes, and Cheswicks did everything impressively.

Miranda plucked a gothic romance from the shelf, surprised to see such a title there. Holding it in her hands, she did a slow tour of the lower shelves, noting the dozens of medical journals, mostly on rare diseases and anatomy. Dr. Astor appeared to be very interested in his field of study and was serious in his pursuit. She wondered what had inspired such dedication. On the carpeted floor by the low burning fire, four books were scattered about. Three were various medical books, one a gothic mystery. Miranda grinned, liking they had a common reading interest. Her father and brother forever berated her on the deplorable books she read, yet there was an intelligent and learned gentleman enjoying the same stories.

The door swung open, and she whirled around, clutching the book to her chest.

Dr. Astor only noticed her after closing the door and strolling halfway across the room. This morning he was dressed with neatness and propriety if not in the first stare of fashion. His hair was still a little over-long, and there was a shadow of a beard along his jawline.

"Pray excuse me, Lady Miranda. If I had had the least suspicion you were here, I shouldn't have dreamt of disturbing you."

He made to leave, and she surged forward. "Please, Dr. Astor, do not leave. This is your home, and I am the intruder."

He turned back to her. "You are my guest," he said with a warm smile. "Not an intruder."

His smile was a sensual assault on her senses. And alarmingly the irresistible beauty of his curved lips made her heart flutter madly. Her reaction last evening had not been an aberration. *How ridiculous you are being, Miranda*! She fiercely berated herself, yet she couldn't help returning his smile.

The doctor ambled over to a large oak desk and chair by the windows and picked up a heavy leather-bound book. A quick glance showed it was a medical journal. Then he selected another from the shelf.

"I shall leave you to the serenity of the library, Lady Miranda." Then with a short bow, he walked toward the door.

She stepped forward. "I wondered, Dr. Astor, how is Tommy this morning?"

He paused with his hand on the doorknob and stared at her in an unflinching, ungentlemanly manner, but what thoughts were running in his head? It would have been impossible for Miranda to guess.

"He is awake with a fierce headache which is to be expected. He is very lucid, and there does not seem to be any swelling around his brain. I have asked his mother to remain my guest for the next few days so I might observe him, then they may continue on their journey."

"I am glad to hear it," she said. "And I do hope for a full recovery soon."

"Mrs. Denniston will be heartened to know you asked. I shall convey your kind wishes." He continued staring at her, and she flushed under his prolonged regard.

"Is there something else, Doctor?" *Why does my heart beat so?*

"I wonder if you might oblige my patients with a spot of reading?"

"And which patients are those?"

"There are five children here. Tommy, William, Little Emma, Lydia, Jasmine, and Serena. I normally read to them, but I have been told recently I would win no accolades in the playhouse."

Miranda laughed lightly. "I would be happy to read to them. Tomorrow as well if they should believe I am up to the task."

"You do not mind? There is a local society here that would be thrilled to have you at their various entertainments."

"I daresay I've had enough parties! I was uncertain what to do with my days while Mamma recovers, and this seems like it would be fun."

"Very well," he murmured, and the appreciative glint in his eyes made her belly flutter in all sorts of odd but thrilling ways. "If you'll follow me, my lady."

He opened the door and sauntered away, and with a smile, Miranda hurried after him, unable to explain her reaction to a man she had no business feeling anything for, even if it was a passing fancy.

Lady Miranda's closeness had a powerful response on Simon's heart. And quite unexplained too. For he'd never had such a reaction to anyone before. Her slender and quite elegant curves were draped in a pale blue cinched-waist gown with a close-fitting bodice trimmed with white lace. She was the possessor of a delicate, heart-shaped face, a pert nose, sharp yet feminine cheekbones, and very sensual lips. Thick lashes framed her extraordinary green eyes, which glowed with bold curiosity whenever she peered at him.

The lady was ravishing, one of the most beautiful he had ever seen. She appeared nothing like the beleaguered miss he'd rescued last evening. Simon felt an unwilling attraction pulse through him as his body reacted with painful immediacy to her lush, sensual beauty. But he ruthlessly denied the attraction, for he'd had intimate pain at the hand of a woman who was beautiful but hid a black, greedy, heart. He wasn't stupid enough to believe all women of such ravishing beauty also held a fickle soul, he however would never allow himself to fall into thrall with a woman because of her physicality. At least not since he was a green lad of one and twenty. It was her character which mattered to him most, though he would allow the kindness he'd seen her display was refreshingly genuine.

"Do the children like music?"

He glanced down at her. "I've never had reason to ask. But I do have a pianoforte. Do you play?"

Her lips curved in a smile and drove the breath from his lungs.

"Superbly," she murmured.

He smiled, noting there was a sadness in her eyes which dimmed her radiance, and he wondered what had put such unhappiness on such a fair countenance. He opened the door to the drawing room, and the children who were on a large carpeted area playing cribbage jerked around and waved wildly.

She touched the sleeve of his jacket, halting him. "I wanted to thank you for your hospitality, Dr. Astor, and for ignoring Mamma's querulousness. I fear whenever in pain, mamma is not as wonderful as I know her to be," she said warmly,

He arched a brow. He mingled enough with those of elevated society to know they did not proffer apologies. How rare and interesting. "I shall bear it in mind."

They made their way to the children who observed their progress with degrees of curiosity.

"Are they all ill?" she asked, sympathy furrowing her brow.

"Yes, but they are in different stages of recovery."

"You've converted your ballroom and larger drawing room into an area to treat your patients. I've never heard of such a thing before. Don't you ever dance?"

"Creating a safe haven for the sick is more important than balls."

She flushed. "I did not mean to imply otherwise. I…I was simply curious about you."

He felt like an eel. "Forgive me," he said with a slight bow. "I have on occasion danced at the local assemblies." And a few balls which his family held. But he kept that information to himself. Many people tended to treat him differently when they realized he was Lord Simon Astor, the third son of a duke. They became unfailingly polite or fawningly pretentious, all hoping to meet the far more important members of his family.

"For many years the people of the village only had an apothecary to rely on for aid. When I finished my last course of study in Edinburgh, I bought this house with a portion of my inheritance from my father. There was a severe outbreak of cholera in the village a few years ago, three to be precise. It was challenging for me to travel to so many houses and patients who needed me each day. I thought it made sense to have them under my roof instead."

He wasn't sure how he felt about the admiration warming her eyes. "It was nothing," he said gruffly. "I was doing my duty."

"I daresay it was more than that," she whispered with a smile. "You made a part of your beautiful home a hospice, not many would be so generous with their wealth and time. I daresay this was more than duty, Dr. Astor."

"What else should I do with so many rooms?" he said with a hint of humor. "I converted the drawing room and the ballroom into comfortable spaces with several beds for those who are too ill to be moved. For the last two years, it is mostly children who occupy those rooms. Critically ill adults are assisted to London for proper care."

They reached the children, and he made swift introductions.

"A real lady?" eleven year-old Lydia demanded with a dubious frown, reaching out to finger the skirt of Lady Miranda's dress. "Like the ones who drive through the parish in their fine dresses and carriages?"

Simon chuckled. "Come now, Lydia, what have I told you about manners?"

She pouted and then smiled shyly at Miranda before dipping into an awkward curtsy. All the children followed Lydia's suit, considering she was the oldest.

Lady Miranda charmed him by returning the honor and sinking into a deep curtsy. "It is a pleasure to meet you all," she said with a broad smile.

Tommy gaped, and Simon entirely sympathized with the boy.

"I was hoping to read to you today," she said, leaning over and plucking the book from his hand.

The children perked up at that and rushed to sit in the center of the carpet. He read to them in that informal style on the ground. "I will drag the sofas and tables over—"

"Please no," she said, tugging off her gloves and dropping them atop one of the side tables. Then she toed off her walking shoes and her stocking-clad toes curled into the soft thickness of the plush carpet. "The floor will do quite nicely."

And it surprised him that something so simple would be enough to beat back the shadows of sadness he had spied earlier. Her green eyes glinting vibrantly, she lowered herself onto the floor, in the center of the children. *What has your life been like, my lady*, he silently wondered.

She opened the book and lowered her voice into a dramatic hush and then started reading. With a smile, he walked away to attend to the other side of his responsibilities, managing his small estate and the several tenants and workers he provided for.

Unexpectedly, he realized he was inordinately glad Lady Miranda would be his guest for two weeks.

CHAPTER 4

Three days after the arrival of his unexpected guests, from the windows of his library, Simon stared in astonishment at the picture before him. Lady Miranda was sprawled on her stomach in the grass by the hidden grotto near the lake, creeping on her knees and belly, a mischievous smile on her face. The sight of that sweet smile filled Simon with an unexpected intense rush of pleasure. He swung the telescope toward the direction she stared and blinked when he saw his wolfhounds crouched, wagging their tails, and staring at her with rabid anticipation. She crept forward, and the blasted dogs mimicked her, meeting her in the middle of the wide-open ground. He wasn't sure if the dogs were acting like her, or if the lady was acting like the dogs. Two of the massive dogs bounded over to her, and she hugged them to her and scratched behind the great brutes' ears, laughing when they tried to slobber on her chin. Simon chuckled at the outrageousness of it all. He stood there for a long time observing the delight she took in something so simple as playing with the animals.

Gripping the telescope in his hands, he left the study and made his way toward the north end section of the estate, where she was hidden in play with the dogs. The lake stretched before them, the sunlight glistening off the water's edge, illuminated the darting fishes below the lake's surface. The dogs sensed his presence and started barking excitedly. She glanced up, pushing a wisp of hair behind her ear. When she saw him, her eyes widened, and a flush ran along her cheeks. How becoming, she appeared, so mussed, and so delightfully improper. Wicked visions of taking her into his arms right here, tumbling her to the grass, and kissing her senseless danced in his mind. Arousal curled like a flame through Simon, and he had to glance away and bring his passions under control.

She surged to her feet, brushing grass and twigs from her dress and hair. Not that it helped, but it did not diminish from her loveliness. Today she'd donned a dark yellow short-sleeved buttoned-up gown where the narrow skirt hugged her slender frame to its best advantage. She had a slim, wild beauty that seemed untouchable, and it amused Simon that she appeared so unconcerned with dirtying her elegant gown. His sister would have squealed with outrage should a spot of mud touched her hemline.

"Have you come to join the puppies and me, Dr. Astor?" she asked with a lift of her chin and a smile on her lips.

"Puppies!" he exclaimed in mock horror. "They are each about ten stones of fully-grown beasts."

She chortled and rubbed behind the ears of Brutus who howled at this pleasure. His large body bounced into hers, and she stumbled. Simon lunged forward and caught her into his arms, and she lifted laughing eyes up to him. The liveliness of her character was enchanting and intoxicating to his senses which had been dormant for years.

"Oh, they are so lovely. I've always wanted a dog or a kitten, but Mamma was allergic to all animals, and they were forbidden."

How wistful she sounded.

"So you decided to sneak away and play with

my dogs, did you?" he asked, dropping his hand from her arms, and moving away. The scent and feel of her was too great a temptation, and it made no sense for him to even try and indulge in a flirtation with her. Refined young ladies like her were not for him. He was the third son, for God's sake. His income was modest, and his inheritance would not last forever. Ladies like Miranda were destined to marry men of impeccable lineage and comfortable fortune. And based on the disposition of her mother and brother, it would also be a family requirement. While his ancestry could live up to the challenge, his wealth would not be sufficient to keep her in the style to which she had long been accustomed.

He'd already used a sizeable chunk of his inheritance to buy this property, and there were no monies to be made from serving the villagers. They paid him in oranges, baked goods, meats, love, and laughter.

Nor could he bear to be a physician to those fine families who could pay him the exorbitant fees most London physicians charged their betters. His services were needed here. Before he had opened his home to those in need, they'd had no one to turn to for medical aid. The apothecary could only do so much, and they had suffered from many diseases with little recourse for support, especially the children.

He had no business wasting his energy thinking about her in a lascivious manner when it was evident to all she was as pure as snow. So even if he had been of a mind to consider seducing her, he would have been the worse sort of libertine to even attempt such a diversion.

"Your mind has gone wandering," she said.

"Pray don't regard it, I fear it happens sometimes." Then he picked up a piece of wood and tossed it.

Sherra, the smallest of the four dogs broke away, and jumped in a beautiful arc, grabbing the stick with her mouth, then proudly trotted over and delivered the stick to Lady Miranda. She laughed and tossed it even further to the dogs' boundless delight for they all raced after the stick. She saw him peeking at her stocking-clad feet and wrinkled her nose.

"Are we taking a walk on the wild and improper side?" he teased drolly.

"Why, I daresay I am!" she said with a cheeky grin, lifting her stained stocking for his inspection. "Mamma would be appalled to see me in such disarray, yet I am quite unconcerned at the thought of her displeasure."

There was that odd wistfulness in her tone once more, and a definite naughty twinkle in her eyes. She bent low and slipped on her walking shoes, then made her way to his side.

"I gather you did not play much as a child."

She smiled. "I had my fair shares of tea parties."

"Did you not run on the grass, roll in the snow, play crickets, and hunt for bugs and beetles? Race on your pony across the lanes of the estate?"

She stared at him in surprise, yearning darkening her eyes. "No," she murmured. "But all those sound lovely except for the searching for bugs and beetles."

He flashed her a grin. "My brothers and even my sister had a grand time at our home in our childhood days. Our childhood was filled with much fun and laughter. Perhaps we were spoilt."

She drifted closer, her soft fragrance of roses and lavender teasing his senses. "Are you the youngest of your siblings?"

He tossed another stick, and this time it was Cronus who bounded after it. "My sister, Lucy, who is recently married, is the youngest at twenty. I am a doddering old man at six and twenty."

"You are remarkably young to be a physician."

"I started studying at sixteen."

The beginning of a smile tipped the corners of her mouth. "How wonderful it must be to be so certain of the path you wish to traverse in life."

He thought about this, surprised to realize he had known years before when he'd first stepped into the Royal College of Physicians, and then moved onto further studies in Glasgow and Edinburgh that he'd wanted to be some healer of sorts. "When I was a lad of eight years, I found a dog on one of our family trips to Brighton. He was half starved, bleeding from many wounds. Perhaps he'd been in a fight, or perhaps his previous owners beat him. I was never certain. My brothers, William and Edward, helped me lift him into our carriage to my mother's great distress," he said with a fond chuckle. "She demanded we let the poor thing out to die, but my father begged her to indulge me. Instead of running in the sand by the seaside or taking to the waters with my family, I was determined to save that dog."

"And did you?"

"To everyone's surprise, including myself, I did.

That dog, whom I named George, went on to live with us for ten years."

She sighed. "I do love happy endings."

"My mother would have preferred if I earned my living as a clergyman. More respectable in her opinion than being a physician."

"From what I have seen, you've acquitted yourself as a physician quite admirably." The gaze she settled on him was piercing, assessing, and with a wicked jolt to his heart, he realized she was attracted to him.

Simon stumbled and silently cursed himself for his clumsiness.

Her lips curved and his fingertips twitched with anticipation of what it would be like to touch her. To kiss her. To walk with her under the banner of stars, to properly court her. All those things she inspired in his heart and more. The lady must be unaware of the captivating picture she made with her smiles, or surely, she would dole them less frequently.

He was flummoxed, for he hardly knew her. It was quite astonishing, the immediacy of which she captured his regard. Simon had never been the type of man to shy away from the things that interested or puzzled him greatly. At his heart, he was scientific, and truly, Lady Miranda invited study. He wanted to get to know her.

Breaking a stick in two, he glanced toward the lowering sun, and the sky painted in a fiery blaze of orange and lavender. "Do you wish to marry?" he asked gruffly.

She broke into a wide, open smile. "I...I do. Once I did not understand the desire my parents had for me to marry. That was all I heard about since I was a child. My eventual come out and the connections I would make with my marriage. And that is all my friends speak about. Who they will walk out with, and when they would marry? For a long time, I became bored with the idea of marriage, certain there was more to life. I would tumble into bed exhausted from late-night balls or rides in the park, and oddly, though I should be having great fun, I started to feel saddened."

At her silence, he prompted, "And?"

"There is more," she murmured. "But there is something beautiful about sharing life experiences and joy with someone who could appreciate all of your eccentricities, is there not? Someone to laugh with, to rest your head upon their shoulder when you are tired. Frequently I would feel lonely at a ball, and I am astonished by that awareness. And it is because I feel I cannot express to my friends what is in my true heart. They might believe me to be a trifle odd for expressing any individuality, but I do believe if one should marry, it should be to someone whom you can be honest about with all your heart."

She chuckled with evident discomfort as if embarrassed about revealing such an intimate part of herself to him. A flash of vulnerability lit in her eyes, and a sudden insight into the sadness in her eyes pierced him. She wasn't allowed to experience life the way she hungered to. Instead, she was guided by her mother's expectations, perhaps even society's, and she wanted to break away without recriminations heaping onto her head.

Unexpectedly she said, "My mamma is determined I wed a prince. As if they pepper London's *haut monde*."

"A genuine prince?"

Her eyes danced with mirth. "But if a prince is unavailable, a duke will do."

In silence they walked farther into the clearing, approaching a small brook.

"Is that what you also wish, to marry a duke?"

"I wish to marry a man I could love," she said softly. "I've been offered for by several gentlemen, but what they admired was my beauty and dowry, but never my intelligence or accomplishments, and most certainly no gentleman has ever truly tried to woo my heart. It seems like such an inconsequential desire—to be liked or even admired by the man I would marry. But when I dwell upon it, what should we talk about if he cannot tolerate me, or if he dislikes my opinions and the way I laugh? There is a rumor in society that Viscountess Bellamy's husband loathes her laugh, comparing it to a braying donkey, and makes every effort to *not* make his wife laugh! He prefers her querulous or simply not to see her at all. Why, I cannot credit it, I hope there is no veracity to the tale. How tedious and painful life would be without genuine affections and caring. I want to be loved…admired…respected for all I am."

Her answer was so unexpected he faltered. She stopped as well, and they faced each other. Simon had never met a young lady of high society who was not determined to snag a gentleman with a title. The entire success of young ladies in the *haut monde* depended on securing an advantageous match, the loftier the title, the better, the more yearly income, the better. Even his sister had made a list of eligible gentlemen to marry with those desirable attributes in her thoughts.

"Mamma, of course, believes I am silly, and Henry says my delicate nerves are overset," she said on an indelicate snort.

He clasped his hands behind his back, lest he tug her into his embrace and did something foolish. "Your desires are perfectly reasonable, and quite admirable if I may say so."

She shot him a surprised but very pleased glance. "I'm gratified to hear you say so."

"I've had such leanings myself."

She arched a brow teasingly. "That you would like to marry a gentleman for love?"

Simon smiled, enjoying her odd humor. He was tempted to inform her that he was the son of a duke, but he did not like how people invariably adjusted their behavior once they learned of his connections to such an elevated family. And it would gut something inside of him if he were to observe such conduct in her. Though he did not believe the lady capable of such hypocrisy.

"I've always thought when I do marry, which I hope to be soon, it must be to a lady who admires me genuinely. And I dare hope she would not choose me because of my income or connections to a distinguished family. I would not begrudge her if she wanted those things, only a fool would wish to live in discomfort and poverty, but I daresay, I hope she would have respect and affections for me."

She turned her head toward him, her eyes brimful of merriment. "You have exactly expressed my feelings. And I daresay if the lady of your heart does not fall madly in love with you, she is a fool." A flash of humor crossed her face. "Perhaps we are a perfect match with all our idealistic idiosyncrasies."

"Alas, I am not a prince," he said, pressing a hand against his chest as if wounded grievously.

"Or a duke," she replied with an unladylike roll of her eyes.

"I could whisk you away to a secret island, where we would marry and live in love for the rest of our days."

Her cheeks pinkened becomingly. "I could tell from your reading books you have a romantic heart."

Simon laughed, reached out, and tucked a wisp of hair behind her ear. "Was it the copy of *Sense and Sensibility* on my desk you saw," he murmured tenderly.

"Isn't the romance between Elinor and Edward simply wonderful."

"I much prefer the sentiments which grew between Colonel Brandon and Maryann."

Lady Miranda rolled her eyes once again, and with much laughter they spent the afternoon on a stroll, discussing the wildly romantic triumph and pitfalls of *Sense and Sensibility*.

CHAPTER 5

Miranda shared a secret smile with Simon across the large breakfast table. Breakfast consisted of tea, a pot of chocolate, toasted bread, strawberry preserves, raisin pastries, coddled eggs, thin slices of ham, and a carrot cake, yet she was not tempted to indulge. There was a hovering sense of something unexpected about to happen in her heart, and it had her stomach in knots.

For the last four days and nights, they had fallen into a routine of taking long walks where they discussed various books and plays, ranging from Shakespeare, Byron, Jane Austen, and even Plato and Socrates. They also discussed Dr. Astor's work, and the fundraising events he hosted from time to time, in the hope of raising funding for a hospital in the area that would serve the people of this village, and of those villages nearby. His selfless giving and passion for helping others filled her heart with remarkable admiration and warmth, and she found that she wanted to assist him in organizing the raising of the money required to build and run the hospital.

And then last night when they had unintentionally met in the library, both unable to sleep, and struck with the similar thought of reading a book. He had read *A Midsummer Night's Kiss*, and she'd curled into a comfortable sofa by the fire and had been lulled by the rich, deep, cadence of his voice. A flutter of warm sensations erupted in her stomach, and her heartbeat quickened uncomfortably at the mere memory of how contented she'd felt.

It saddened her to realize she would depart his home soon, as her mother was eager to leave for their country home in Lincolnshire where they would retire until next season.

"Dr. Astor, Miranda mentioned in passing that you have siblings. Do they not live here with you?" her mother asked, not content to eat in silence.

Henry crunched his toast noisily, quite uncharacteristic of him, for propriety was just as important to him as it was to Mamma. Miranda suspected he was intolerably bored and anything was a diversion. She had caught him yesterday flirting with the young housekeeper, who had been blushing like a silly, fresh faced debutante.

Simon slowly spread the strawberry preserve over his cake. "My sister is married and living within her own household. My older brothers have both been away from England for the last five years. William is in India and Edward in New York. And my mother has not left Hampshire since our father went onto his reward seven years ago."

"You are comfortably situated for a third son," the countess said with considerable inquisitiveness. "Should I know of your family, Dr. Astor?"

Before he could reply, the door to the breakfast parlor opened and Mrs. Denniston, suitably attired in a blue frock, strolled inside. "I was checking in on my Tommy, or I would have been down when the bell rang," she said with a tentative smile.

The countess had been taking trays in her room and previously had no occasion to dine with everyone these last few nights. Miranda hadn't thought it any of her mother's concern to mention the lady was still in residence, and her mother had not enquired after the boy.

"Is she to dine with us?" she demanded in evident outrage.

Exasperated, Miranda set down her teacup with an uncharacteristic *thud*. "Mamma!"

"Dr. Astor, I expect a man of your standing to—"

"You will have no expectations of me or anyone I've invited to my home and table, Lady Langford. I do, however, expect all my guests to be treated with cordiality and for each person in my home to be mindful of their tongue and manners."

Mrs. Denniston had frozen, but now her shoulders relaxed, and she bobbed a quick thanks to Simon before taking a seat, which he stood and held out for her. Henry choked on his tea, his eyes widening, never once having heard anyone reprimanding Mamma. The countess's lips pinched, and a flush worked itself along her elegant cheekbones. Then she visibly composed herself.

The echo of running footsteps sounded, and the breakfast parlor doors were once more flung open. Mrs. Clayton rushed inside; her face flushed from exertion. "Dr. Astor, a cart with a young lady just pulled inside the forecourt." She glanced at everyone, before saying, "There is blood, Sir! I fear there might have been a horrible accident."

He pushed back his chair and surged to his feet. "If you will all excuse me."

Mrs. Denniston had also stood. "Might I be of assistance?"

He nodded. "Thank you. Most of the staff are out for their off day, and I've been known to rely on a helping hand from a maid or two."

They hurried from the room, and Simon broke into a run.

Her stomach twisted in tight, painful knots. "It must be serious," Miranda said. "Did you hear that, Mamma? She arrived on a cart, and there was blood."

"Young lady, you will sit and resume our breakfast."

It was then she realized she had pushed out her chair. "Mamma!" Miranda cried, aghast. Her frantic gaze volleyed to Henry. "Surely they could use as much help as possible. Mrs. Clayton said the accident was horrible and Dr. Astor might be overwhelmed."

Her mother wrinkled her nose in distaste. "I am certain there was no one of consequences on that coach, my dear, there is no need to be anxious and to risk your reputation and safety by even thinking of helping! I am sure the good doctor will have sufficient help in his servants."

"Well said, Mamma," Henry said, then with shocking unconcern he snapped the pressed newssheet open and started to read.

Her mother could be intolerably blunt and unfeeling to those she deemed lower, but this was beyond the pale. Unable to bear their indifference, she pushed from the table and hurried away, disregarding the cries of her mother. She made her way to the drawing room door and gently opened it up. The slight metallic tang of blood reached Miranda instantly. She hesitated on the threshold, before firming her shoulders and stepping inside, and closing the door behind her. A lady reposed on one of the beds sobbing, the sound raw and pain-filled. It propelled Miranda forward, and she halted when she saw the high mound pushing up on her gown.

The lady was with child.

"I need three basins of hot water," Simon snapped to a hovering servant, propping several pillows behind the lady, and easing her into a sitting position. "Clean towels and linens and carbolic soap immediately!"

"Yes, Doctor!"

The maid hurried away with Mrs. Denniston accompanying her to assist.

Simon glanced up, his face a mask of fierce concentration. "Lady Miranda?" he asked sharply. "Is something wrong?"

"No…I…. The coachman has gone to the village for more help?"

He nodded. "There is a midwife there with whom I work closely, he has gone to fetch her." He shifted back to the lady and murmured, "Come now, Sarah, all will be well. I'll ensure it. The child is ready to come into this world."

"I'm afraid, Doctor, she gasped," tears streaming down her face. "I fear something is wrong. No pain should be this great." Then deep wrenching sobs tore from the woman.

A sinking sensation entered Miranda's stomach. Was the woman dying? Miranda's heart pounded a fierce rhythm, and she wanted to run away, but she kept herself rooted. "Is there anything I can do to help, Simon?"

Her voice trembled.

"This is no place for you, but thank you for the offer."

Relief scythed through her heart and she made to turn away. Shame also rushed in, for it was evident he needed assistance with most of his servants out on their half day. Her sensibilities felt shattered, and she could not explain why she felt so frightened. The poor woman must be suffering from such palpitations. Squaring her shoulders, and praying for courage, she skirted around the bed, careful only to look at the lady's face. She pushed one of the wingback chairs close to the bedside, sat, and reached for the lady's hand. This much closer to the lady, she noted the air smelled thick with sweat and blood.

Simon glanced up, paused momentarily in surprise, before giving her a quick, pleased smile. Then he went back to peering under the woman's skirt. Mortification flushed through Miranda, and she felt the writhing lady possibly endured a similar embarrassment.

"What is your name?" she asked soothingly.

"Sarah, milady," she gasped, gripping onto Miranda's hand with surprising strength. The lady wailed, her body contorting.

Miranda felt faint. Surely this could not be what all women suffered to bring a child into this world? She murmured soothing words and stroked the damp hair from her head. "What will you name your child?"

"Victoria, milady, for our queen."

"It is a girl then?"

An unexpected smile lit her face. "I do hope so, milady."

"Please, you may call me Mira...or Miranda if you prefer."

"Thank you—" she broke off on a sharp scream.

Miranda kept her eyes glued to the lady's face, not daring to look anywhere else. The maid and Mrs. Denniston returned with jugs of water and towels, and Simon moved away to scrub his hands quite roughly with the block of carbolic soap.

"Ughhhh," Sarah whimpered.

"Hush now, it shall soon be over," Miranda murmured, praying that was true.

Sweat ran in rivulets down her hairline, and her face was a grimace of agony. At that moment a contraction seized Sarah's body, and she crushed Miranda's hand. But she bore it, gritting her teeth at times through the pain, other moments murmuring soothing nonsense, and patting Sarah's forehead with a fresh, damp towel.

Simon guided Sarah with calming words and, at times, sharp instructions on when to push, and when to breathe. It felt like it went on forever, and even Miranda started to sweat, for the tendrils of her hair clung damply to her cheeks and nape. Sarah's screams and low, guttural moans caused panic to coil around Miranda's lungs, tightening until she could not breathe.

Finally, a sharp cry echoed through the room, and Miranda glanced down and gulped. The tiniest, reddest human she had ever seen with white and red bits all about thrashed around in the doctor's hands. Dr. Astor was doing a great job of cleaning away the mess with a soft wet, warm towel. Then he bundled the baby in an even softer blanket and handed the baby over to the now joyously weeping mother.

Miranda felt fit for Bedlam, she was uncertain how Sarah could now be laughing as if she held the greatest happiness in the world in the cradle of her arms. Emotions clogged Miranda's throat, and her heart pounded a fierce beat she did not understand. Standing on legs which felt weakened, she hurried from the room unable to speak. She had been in the room where a lady had given birth. Who among her friends would have thought her capable of such feats?

She felt Dr. Astor's piercing stare as his gaze followed her, she broke into a run, skidding to a

A PRINCE OF MY OWN

frantic halt to wrench the door open, and then closing it gently behind her. Leaning against it, she closed her eyes tightly. "Oh God, I must tell Pippa," she gasped. "In truth, I must warn every friend of mine."

Miranda hurried into the smaller parlor, grateful to see it was empty, desperate to compose herself and try to understand the emotions tearing through her. The pianoforte beckoned, and she went over and lifted the well-polished lid. She allowed her fingers to dance over the keys, creating soft chiming music. The sound of it grounded her, and she lightly played, allowing the keys and the music to be her center.

The door swung open, and she whirled around. "Dr. Astor!"

"Simon...," he said, staring at her intently. "I daresay we can be informal with each other, Miranda."

How tenderly he said her name as if he savored the shape and sound of it on his lips.

"I would like that, Simon," she said softly, appalled at her bursting into tears.

In a few strides, he was before her, lightly touching her shoulder.

"That was a brave, kind thing you did,

Miranda," he said with a slow smile that touched somewhere deep inside her. "Thank you. Sarah is just as thankful and hoped you will see baby Victoria before you leave."

Miranda nodded, unable to speak past the knot of emotions tightening her throat. Finally, she said, "I never knew having a child was painful. I am mortified to have been so ignorant, and I daresay if women knew, surely, they would not anticipate marriage and children with such blind expectations. Why has Mamma never told me?"

The harshness of his expression softened. "In my experience, most women do not regret that pain afterward and anticipate having more children."

He shifted scandalously closer to her, and unable to explain the needs rioting through her, she pressed into his arms. Simon did not hesitate or display shock at her lack of propriety, his hands came around her waist like bands of steel, pulling her into the hard, masculine heat of his body. She was surrounded by his clean male scent, and it felt so right to be held in his arms.

They stood like that for several moments, until the erratic beat of her heart quieted to a semblance of normalcy. Blushing at her lapse, she pulled away from him, absently massaging the ache in her fingers and wrist.

He leaned forward and encircled her wrist and brought it up for inspection. "Sarah's grip must have been painful. You are bruised. I'll rub some ointment for you. It will ease the ache and reduce the swelling." Then he brushed the lightest kiss across her inner wrist. The action seemed to surprise him more than it did her and, with a soft curse which caused her ears to burn, he stepped back.

The pit of her stomach felt strange, fluttery, and warmth slid through her veins. "I...I...thank you for allowing me to be a part of the experience," she said huskily, painfully aware she did not pull her fingers from his hand.

His gaze flickered briefly to her mouth, and her heart clamored. *He wants to kiss me*, Miranda realized with a sense of shock. The air tightened with an unexpected tension, and her belly fluttered as if a thousand birds had taken flight.

"Simon...I...I...."

"Yes?"

Her senses felt assaulted by his scent and the burning need glowing from his blue gaze. The fierce intensity with which his eyes devoured her frame had both natural reticence and desire coursing through her veins. She was at a loss to explain anything, for she did not understand the twisting ache sliding through her body. The desire to touch him, to kiss his lips was as overwhelming as it was inexplicable.

He cupped her cheeks with both hands, tilting her head up, using one of his thumbs to swipe across her lower lip in a soft, sensual caress. "Thank you for being brave and so kind to a stranger. Many would not have thought it or retained such admirable composure."

Her breath hitched at his fervent whisper and the shadows of hunger in his eyes, and she swallowed at the startling throb in her lower belly. He dipped his head slowly, giving her enough time to retreat. Miranda stood frozen, anticipation trembling through her heart with wicked fierceness. At this moment she was unable to care about duty to her mother's expectations. She had never been kissed before, never allowed an ardent suitor to steal any moments, only because none had ever tempted her heart to misbehave.

He pressed a tender kiss to the corner of her mouth, and her knees weakened. She grasped his shoulder, steadying herself. His mouth took hers in a ravishing kiss yet infused with such gentleness her throat ached. It was a kiss that offered comfort, for she still shivered in reaction to what she had witnessed. It was a kiss which communicated want and stunning hunger, a kiss that gave and took in equal measures.

With a soft groan, she parted her lips at his urging. He slanted his lips over hers, drawing a moan of pure need from the depths of her being. The rasping glide of his tongue against hers nearly drove Miranda to her knees. She stood on her toes, sinking further into his wild kiss, losing herself and blindly twining her fingers through the hair curling at the nape of his neck. His mouth settled more possessively over hers, his tongue urging her lips to part wider to his incredible sensual assault.

His hands stroked her jaw, over to her collarbone, down to the underside of her breast, and stayed there. Flames of desire consumed her, and she sobbed wildly into his intimate embrace. Her breasts felt peculiar, they were suddenly heavy and full, her nipples tautening into almost painful sensitivity. How clever he was with his mouth. How wickedly delightful. How lovely and everything she had ever thought a kiss could be. He caught her lower lip between his teeth and suckled it.

With a muffled groan of regret, he released her mouth. He pulled from her, littering small kisses across her cheek, then to her forehead where he lingered. He pressed kisses along her cheek, and neck, down to her neckline where he inhaled deeply. He shuddered in her arms before releasing her and stepping back. "Lady Miranda, forgive me—"

"Do not apologize," she whispered fiercely, peering up at him. "That was my very first kiss, and I thank you for making it so wonderful."

"Your first kiss?" he asked with gruff and pleased incredulity.

"Yes," she said with a small smile which trembled.

"I thank you for the honor of it." They stared at each other for several moments, a perilous tension heavy on the air.

Then he bowed, turned around and left. Miranda collapsed on the sofa and pressed her face into her palms.

Oh, what have I done?

CHAPTER 6

Miranda had dreamt of Simon kissing her and doing far more to her than she had ever imagined being possible. It had appalled her that her subconscious could have betrayed her in such a manner, for her dreams had been wickedly delightful. She had been roused from slumber with her heart pounding, and an unfulfilled ache she did not understand.

"Oh, how intolerably bored I am," Countess Langford groused, glaring at her feet propped high atop the cushions.

"The report from Dr. Astor was good, Mamma," Miranda said with a comforting smile as she looked over from the canvas before her. "You'll be on your feet in no time. Would you like me to continue reading?"

Her mamma leaned back on the chaise with a sigh. "I've had enough of Shakespeare for the day. Your poor father must be in such a worry to have us home with him." A tiny frown appeared between her winged brows. "Agnes has informed me you've been taking long walks with Dr. Astor these past few days."

Miranda's heart fluttered wildly in her breast. "Yes," she said, inordinately glad she faced away from her mamma. Surely, she would have seen the guilt in her eyes and the flush on her cheeks. "The doctor is very charming company, and I do enjoy our long walks. I am quite aware of Agnes following at a discreet distance, Mamma. I am properly chaperoned if that is your worry."

She felt her mother's stare, but she concentrated on her brushstrokes, as she painted the view of the estate visible through the large windows of the parlor.

"Need I remind you that as the daughter of an earl, it would be unseemly for you to form an attachment with a man inferior to your rank and wealth?"

"The reminder is not necessary, Mamma, I've been told every day since I was twelve years of age." She lowered the brushes to the side table and stood. "If you'll excuse me, I promised the children I would read to them today. Three of them are going home."

Her mother considered her with a critical eye, before nodding once.

Miranda left the parlor and walked to the drawing room where the children were gathered playing cribbage.

"Lady Miranda!" they chorused. "Join us!"

She tumbled to the carpet and played with them for more than an hour. They all seemed more robust, their skin a healthy pink, their eyes enlivened with happiness. She spent a good portion of the afternoon with them reading and playing cards, and even gathering them together for a quick sketch of a portrait.

Shortly after luncheon, Simon returned from his jaunt to the village. Nerves coursed through her as he approached her where she reposed under a beech tree with her canvas, easel, and paintbrush. A breeze rustled through the top branches of the trees and swept along the mowed grass bringing a scent of roses and pines. The memory of the way he had kissed her sent a dizzying thrill through her.

She watched him approach, trying to affect a mien of polite inquiry. He was so very handsome, with the firm set of his chin, piercing eyes, and sensually firm lips. His tan riding breeches fitted splendidly to his lean waist, powerful thighs, and long muscular legs. His jacket and waistcoat molded quite closely to his broad shoulders.

Since their kiss yesterday, she'd not seen Simon. Something about him—she had no idea what—evoked confusing emotions within her. Perhaps it was this hunger she had inside to know everything about him, even as she sensed such a desire to be futile.

Her family would not accept a man of such an inferior rank to be her husband. So, she should view their outings as a brief bit of harmless fun, a brief flirtation, and a pleasant diversion. But she could not prevent the leanings of her heart, even though she had spent hours staring at the ceiling this morning, reminding her heart and mind to be cautious.

Each time his gaze touched hers, her heart trembled in response. Miranda was falling for the doctor, and she did not know how to stop it. Worse, she did not want to halt the sense of belonging she felt at his side.

He sketched a bow, his eyes never leaving her face. "Good afternoon, Lady Miranda."

"Good afternoon, Dr. Astor."

They stared at each other, and both laughed at the same time, dispelling the tension which had wound itself around her heart. "Are we to be frightfully civil to each other?" she asked, chuckling.

He removed his hat and slapped it against his thigh. "Absolutely not. Would you like to take a ride with me?"

She glanced at the carriage parked along his well-maintained gravel driveway. "In your carriage?"

His stare was a tangible thing, reaching to touch her, warming her in places she hadn't known were cold. "On horses."

She scrambled to her feet, he reached out and assisted her up. "I would be most delighted! It would take me a few minutes to change into a riding habit."

"It would be my pleasure to wait for you."

With a laugh, she hurried away, calling for Agnes once she reached inside the manor. Miranda was glad she had thought to pack a riding habit for the long-forgotten weekend party. She quickly donned a dark blue buttoned-up shirt and half jacket, a skirt, and riding boots, and made her way back to Simon.

He now awaited her with two beautiful horses—a chestnut filly and a black stallion.

"They are so very lovely," she breathed, strolling up to the chestnut and patting her down. "Oh, you, wonderful beauty," she crooned. "I shall enjoy riding you."

Simon choked, and she glanced over at him. "Is all well?"

He had the oddest glint in his beautiful eyes. "Are you ready to race my brave, intrepid lady?"

"A race!"

"Why not?"

Miranda chuckled. "Are you certain you wish to race me, Simon? I am an expert horsewoman, you know."

"Ah, a challenge I cannot refuse."

The earlier gentle breeze strengthened. "How far do we ride?" she asked securing her hat firmly atop her curls.

"Until that sad uncertainty I see in your eyes melts away. Feel the sun on your skin, the wind on your cheeks, the power of the horse underneath you, and leave your cares behind you."

Miranda stared at him for a long silent moment. "Then let's race."

He encircled her waist from behind and assisted her onto her horse. She flushed at the intimate proximity. His eyes darkened with the knowledge, causing her heartbeat to intensify. He mounted his stallion, and they cantered away. They did not speak, just rode with the wind.

The earth shook with the power of their horses, and she laughed in exhilaration at the magnificent speed and grace of the animals. Simon did not hold back, he urged his horse ahead of hers with such grace and elegance he stole her breath. Like her, he did not use a whip, but bent low over his horse, speaking encouraging words to urge him to greater speed. Joy pumped through her veins, and her heartbeat quickened as they sped past the rolling countryside, a blur of greens and the bright splash of flowers and roses.

The steady sounds of hoof beats thumping the ground in a thrilling rhythm urged her to encourage her horse to move faster. They cut the corner at breakneck speed, and delight pulsed through her veins. The power of his stallion outdistanced hers, but she did not care, and soon they came to a stop.

"Simon, we must do this again tomorrow! That was so very exhilarating. I declare I am unable to ride with such freedom in Hyde Park."

"I thought you would enjoy the wind on your face."

A wild desire to leap from the horse and kiss him darted through her. Unable to help herself, her fingers drifted to her lips and ghosted over them remembering the firm pressure of his mouth on hers, the evocative taste of his tongue sliding against hers. Flushing at her thoughts, she glanced away. She jumped from the horse without his assistance, and he arched an admiring brow. He dismounted with effortless grace, and holding onto the horse's reins, they began to stroll without any particular goal in mind.

A soft, misting rain began to fall, and she tilted her face to the sky briefly. "We should return inside," she said softly, smoothing a stray wisp of a curl from her temple.

When he made no reply, she glanced at him and faltered. He stared at her with a question in his gaze. The sudden tension in him was palpable, and his eyes darkened with dangerous heat. A surge of heightened awareness went through her.

"You are breathtaking, and I do not refer to your beauty. You are so much more."

She stood still, her hands at her sides curled into fists to keep from touching him. Something deep within her belly quickened, sending powerful darts of longing through her. He dipped his head and tenderly kissed her forehead. A lump grew in her throat and tears pricked behind her lids.

The sound of thundering hooves in the distance had Simon shifting with a frown.

"It is Jim," he murmured. "Something must have happened for him to ride me down out here."

The coachman arrived, chest heaving. "It is David Belmont, the blacksmith. Dr. Astor. He is complaining of stomach pain. He's fevered and casting up his accounts. They fear…" the man glanced away, a line of strain bracketing his mouth.

"Forgive me, Miranda, I must tend to my patient immediately. Might I ask Jim to accompany you back to the house?"

She nodded, and he vaulted on his horse and rode away with thundering speed.

. . .

A LITTLE OVER AN HOUR LATER, Miranda had changed into one of her most serviceable gowns and made her way toward the drawing room. She wanted to offer her assistance to Simon in the event he might need more help. Upon her return from riding, she had learned someone from the village had carted the blacksmith to the manor, and he was currently in the drawing room. She knocked once and entered the room. Simon was bent over a groaning man, and there was an air of tension within the room.

She made no sound, but somehow, he sensed her presence and glanced up.

A fierce scowl settled over his features. "Get out of here!" he snapped his eyes flashing.

She was taken so much by surprise that she could only stare at him, "I've come to help," she said firmly. "What might I do? Please instruct me."

"I said get out!" he roared with such violence she jerked as if slapped.

A horrified gasp came from the young man assisting him, and he sent her a sympathetic glance. Embarrassment burning through her, she turned around, wrenched the door open and darted away.

ALMOST TWO HOURS LATER, Simon stepped from the bath where he had thoroughly scrubbed himself on the odd chance his patient was afflicted with nothing more than a case of tainted meat. An odd urgency coiled in his gut. The wounded look in Miranda's eyes made him feel like the worst sort of bounder, and he had to find her right away. Dressing without the aid of his valet, he hurried from his chamber and down the winding stairs into the hallway.

Mrs. Clayton who had been ambling toward the servant's staircase paused and considered him. "Lady Miranda ran toward the lake, Doctor, and has not returned. I am assuming it is she you wish to see?"

He nodded his thanks, and made his way outside, into the crisp evening air. He hurried toward the lake, and several moments later, released a sigh of relief to find her lying on the grass, unconcerned with the damage to her dress. Miranda had removed the pins from her hair, and the most glorious golden blonde tresses he'd ever seen were spread about her head and shoulders on the verdant grass.

Simon lowered himself beside her, aware that the slight hill behind of them would hide them from the view of the main house and anyone looking out their windows.

"I am sorry," he said gruffly, laying back on the grass, and staring at the lowering sun. "I did not want to risk you and when I saw you enter that door…I felt afraid."

She shifted her head, and he felt her stare. "Afraid of what?" she murmured.

"I thought the symptoms might be cholera. A most ravaging disease which always invariably leads to death. When I thought of you near it…I reacted." He turned his head to face her. "You are precious to me, Miranda."

The silence which fell between them was fraught with intimate peril. Simon fingered strands of her hair and relished their cool softness against his knuckles. He pushed to his feet and held out his hand. Trustingly, she placed her fingers within his, he tugged her to her feet and led her behind an arbor of trees.

Then he leaned in and pressed a soft kiss against her lips. They stood together, mouth to mouth, in almost shocked amazement of their incredible daring. A doctor kissing the daughter of an earl. A beauty unlike any he'd ever seen, a woman destined to marry a duke or a prince. Not a third son.

Pushing all those misgivings aside, he drew her closer, flushing her body against his. He thrust his fingers into her hair, which ran like a waterfall over his skin, a sensual delight to the touch. Simon kissed her, unable to halt the desire roaring through his body for her. And she responded with shivering waves of sensuality. They kissed over and over, until her lips appeared red and swollen, her eyes glazed with passion.

"I want to court you, Miranda."

Her breath hitched, and her eyes widened. "I want that too." Then she closed her eyes. " Mamma will never agree to me accepting a proposal from you."

"I am not without connections," he replied. "I have an inheritance of five thousand pounds a year.

And I daresay we will never want for a supply of fruits, farm produce, baked goods and similar from my patients."

She choked back her laughter, but her eyes danced with merriment.

"I will speak to your father," he said gruffly.

She nodded, though there was a deep glow of uncertainty in her gaze.

"I'll fight for you," he vowed.

A broad smile bloomed on her lips, and she sank into his embrace.

Soothingly against his chest, she said, "I'll fight for you too, Simon." And though the words were muffled, they pierced him deep inside.

And that was enough for today.

CHAPTER 7

Simon strolled along the lawns of his estate, his hands clasped behind his back, a sense of peace and happiness pervading his veins. Miranda walked beside him, the picture of loveliness. But it was the soft smile of contentment upon her lips which filled him with a queer sense of joy. That empty, hollow glaze which had lingered in her eyes had vanished, and it was replaced by a look that was so tender and sweet, it gave him hope when he should be cautious.

"Your mother is quite fit to travel. I've informed her so myself early this morning. Today is to be her last day of bedrest, and she is quite eager to depart my dreadfully boring manse."

Miranda winced. "I apologize for Mamma's tongue."

Simon grinned. "All patients are dreadfully bored and intolerably odious when confined to a bed."

"You are too kind," she said with a light laugh.

She bit into her lower lip, a nervous gesture.

"I have hopes to travel this weekend to visit your father at the country home, where I will speak to him about courting you."

"He will be home. Papa is the master of the hunt, and I daresay hunting is all he had been anticipating for the season. He finds balls and most of the *ton* intolerably boring, you know."

Simon cleared his throat. "My brother is a duke."

Miranda faltered and stared at him in astonishment. "Good gracious!" she exclaimed involuntarily.

"My brother has been away from England for several years, and though he writes me often, he does not mention any plans to return to our shores soon. His estates are managed by his stewards and lawyers. Despite our family's absence from *ton* life for several years, I am hoping that connection would allow your father to grant us his blessings."

"Papa is very complacent to Mamma's wishes," Miranda said faintly. "And I fear she would not be happy with any circumstance that does not see me marrying into a title." She took a deep breath. "Perhaps we *should* run away," she said with a laugh that did not reach her eyes. "I am over one and twenty, and my birthday is in less than six weeks."

"We'll not start a scandal," he murmured, though he could not say what he would not do to make her his.

She gave him an impish grin and looped her hands with his and leaned into his side. "We shall host many fundraising balls together for the hospital. And perhaps a festive ball for the villagers each year? Do you have a London townhouse?"

"I do, though I believe we will have to get a bigger one. My bachelor residence in Russell Square is not up to scratch."

"Hmm, that can be easily rectified. And perhaps six children."

He choked on air. "Six!"

She sent him a wide-eyed innocent glance. "Too little or too many?"

They laughed, and the love that clutched at his heart was unlike any he'd ever felt.

"Simon?"

He peered down at her. "Yes?"

"From your fine manners and wealth, I suspected you belonged to a well-connected family, but why did you not tell me that you are the son of a duke?"

"It was foolish of me," he said gruffly. "I felt perhaps our interactions would have been different."

She stared up at him. "Perhaps, I am certain Mamma would have been less difficult and far more charming. And would have insisted on meeting your brother immediately! But it is of little consequence to me, only in that it gives me hope that Mamma will be more receptive of an alliance between our families."

Stone paths guided the way toward a green hedgerow maze while stone seats invited repose and admiration of the beautiful lake in the distance. He led her toward the bench near a small brook and lowered himself onto it. Instead of urging her to sit beside him, he tugged her onto his thigh, and a look of scandalized amusement settled on her lovely face.

"Once I loved a girl, or believed I did."

"Oh!"

"Hmm," he said, pushing a loose tendril from her chignon behind her ear. The unruly curl popped right back out. "I was one and twenty at the time, and believed I would marry Miss Phoebe Cranston, the daughter of a viscount. I presented her to my family who approved the match, but for her…it was all about using me to get closer to my brother, who has the title."

She winced. "Oh Simon, I am so terribly sorry. Did your brother marry her?"

"He did not, though he very nearly well did. William did not love her, but he believes in honor and duty. It was his luck our mamma was in the conservatory and witnessed it all when Miss Phoebe tried to compromise him."

Miranda touched his mouth with trembling fingers. "Your heart must have been so disillusioned after."

"Only for a few months," he murmured.

"There is something I must tell you." The unexpected tears in her eyes jolted his heart with alarm.

"What is it, Miranda?"

"I…I tried to compromise a duke once by slipping into his room at a garden party!" Shame darkened her eyes, and a flush mounted on her cheeks. She closed her eyes as if bracing against his disgust.

"I am delighted you failed."

Her eyes flew open. "You do not sound angry."

He kissed her, a simple meeting of lips, an exchange of breath, without demand. "I only admire your braveness and honesty."

She wilted against him, pressing her forehead against his shoulder. "I've apologized to him and his lovely wife, who is also my dearest friend, but I still feel wretched with shame whenever I recall it. I wanted to be his duchess, not because I admire the man himself, but because I desired his title and I was getting impatient for him to be captivated. And I knew I would have made Mamma very proud."

He placed a finger under her chin and lifted her face to his. Using his thumb, he wiped away the tear which had rolled down her cheek. "You are too hard on yourself, my sweet. You took responsibility for your mistakes and affected an apology. There is no shame in that. You've acquitted your honor quite well."

She turned her face and pressed a kiss into his palm. "You have a remarkable gift for always making my heart happy," she said with a sweet shyness. "Thank you, Simon."

A whisper of a kiss feathered over his jaw, and he closed his eyes against the sensations. "I want to stay here and kiss you until we are both senseless with desire, but I must call upon the squire to see how he fares. He broke his damn leg trying to fox hunt."

She slipped her hand around his neck, the wicked temptress teasing him with another kiss on his chin. Then their mouths met, and the fire of desire drowned his senses. Holding her close to his chest, Simon tenderly ravished her mouth with long, heart-pounding kisses. His lips devoured hers, and he stroked his tongue in her mouth with ruthless persuasion. Unable to stop touching her, he explored her mouth thoroughly, and the onslaughts of sensations were overwhelming.

She tasted of sweetness and fire, of innocence and wantonness. Each kiss went deeper, lingered longer, communicating lust, tenderness, and such burning love. His cock hardened on a fierce pulse of desires, and he had to beat back the raw need demanding he lift her and place her on the soft grass to make love with her. With a ragged groan, Simon pulled from her, littering small kisses across her cheek. He bit the curve of her throat, fighting the raging need to devour her.

"Simon!" she gasped, shivering in his arms.

He slid his hand along the curves of her thighs, worshipping the feel of her sweet, slender body, up to her hips. Lifting his head, he stared at her. "When I release you, run away from me and do not look back."

The pulse fluttered at the base of her throat, her skin flushed, and her eyes had deepened to forest green. "And if I do not?"

"Then I will kiss you *everywhere* until you are wet and desperate for me, then I'll take your virtue, right here with the sun beating down on us."

An inarticulate murmur slipped from her. Instead of being afraid at the sensual threat, his wicked minx boldly thrust her fingers through his hair and took his mouth with shocking carnality. The kiss was over before it began, and she jerked to her feet and hurried away, the wind carrying her soft laughter back to him.

SEVERAL HOURS LATER, Simon was bent over his medical journal, scribbling his observances noting in patients with symptoms which suggested they might have future problems with their health. He made it his duty, to carefully record his cases, the symptoms, the care he suggested, and their improvements or lack thereof. The door to the library swung open, but he did not lift his head. Thinking it to be his housekeeper who normally peeked in at this time of the day with a tray for him to eat, he muttered, "I'll be right with you, Mrs. Clayton."

"Is that the greeting I'm to receive after six years?" a low voice murmured.

Simon snapped his head up, the breath whooshing from his lungs. "Speak of the devil!"

His brother's dark blue eyes, very much like his own lit up with amusement. "Ah, speaking of me, earlier were you?"

Simon grinned, blotting the journal and lowering his quill. "Only this morning." He stood and bounded around the large desk to meet his brother in the center of the room. They hugged fiercely, and Simon was surprised to feel a lump forming in his throat.

"I missed you," he said gruffly. "Why didn't you send word that you were coming?"

"I missed you too," his brother replied, slapping him on his back.

They pulled apart, and William dragged his fingers through his short-cropped hair. "I fancied I would arrive before my letter. But surely you expected me after your last letter informing me that Mamma is slipping into an ever-deeper state of melancholia."

Simon strolled over to the side table, lifted a decanter filled with whisky and poured two glasses. He handed one to his brother who took it with an expression of rich pleasure.

"Mother has been in Bath these last four months. She has bought a house in Camden Place and there is a sly rumor about town that she has the peculiar interest of a viscount ten years her junior. Her letters are filled with more cheer and good humor of late, but I daresay she will be thrilled to have you home."

William nodded and sipped his drink. "I received a letter from Edward some six months ago, that he is getting married, to an American, and he means to bring her home for the family to meet her."

"I received one too. Mother will be well pleased to have all of us once again under her roof."

William ambled over to the sofa by the fireplace and lowered himself into its plush depth. "And little Lucy?"

"Not so little anymore, and not of a mind to

forgive you for missing her wedding. You have a lot to make up for with your absence."

"That I do," he murmured.

Simon took in the changes in his brother. He seemed tougher, the dark swarthiness of his skin a testimony he spent most of his hours under the sun. Nor was he dressed in clothes befitting a duke with considerable estates and wealth, but in a manner of casual disregard of his station. He was dressed in dark trousers and an open-neck white linen shirt.

"It is very good to have you home, William. Though I do not believe Mamma's melancholia is the only reason you've returned home."

William took a healthy swallow of his drink. "I mean to marry. Fulfill my duties and obligations to the title."

Simon stilled. "Are you certain?"

William had loved a girl once, and she had fallen ill. He hadn't been the same amusing, carefree brother after, and it hadn't been long before he had run all the way from England.

A dark shadow shifted in his brother's eyes before he buried the raw flare of emotions. "Sophia is gone, I've accepted that. I…I long for another voice to listen to and perhaps share my cares."

"I am sorry I wasn't able to save her," Simon

said softly, his heart pounding a fierce beat. "I've waited almost six years to tell you that. I did not want to say it in a damn letter."

William flinched, and an emotion akin to despair flashed in the depths of his eyes. "Did you believe I could ever blame you? Cholera ravaged her village, and there was nothing you could have done about it. Nothing! If anyone was at fault, it is me for not marrying her sooner and taking her away from there. I allowed anxiety in my heart because of the differences in our circumstances and the duty I had to my station.

His brother tugged at his non-existent cravat, and Simon sensed the walls which numerous times he had stated close on him unexpectedly, once again made their presence known.

"Let's take a walk on the estate grounds and catch up on everything."

William stood, and downed the contents of his glass in a long swallow. Simon followed suit, and then they made their way outside, despite the slow drizzle of rain. He was glad his brother was home, yet there was a disquieting sensation filling his gut, which was as inexplicable as it was strange. Pushing it aside, he strolled with his brother as they caught up on the last six years.

CHAPTER 8

Miranda sat in the smaller parlor, painting the scenery she'd seen from her chamber—a picturesque lake, surrounded by large oak and willow trees, swans gliding above the water, and birds flitting and twittering about—folding it perfectly with the view she'd had earlier.

"Miranda! Miranda! Come quickly, girl! Where are you?" the countess called, her tone throbbing with excitement.

Caught up in her work, she attempted to brush aside her mother's stringent calls, much as she had done the luncheon gong earlier.

"Miranda!"

With a sigh, she lowered the paintbrush, stood, and tugged off the apron. Hurrying toward the door, she wondered what had gotten her mother in such a state of excitable nerves. Only yesterday she had been morose and lamenting staying another day under the boring doctor's roof who associated with such undesirables. She glided down the curving staircase to see her mother exiting from the parlor. The countess glanced up, and a broad smile bloomed on her lips. Miranda was startled at the speed with which she hobbled on her still tender ankle. Not wanting her mamma to fall, she hurried down to meet her. "Mamma, what is happening?"

"Come, girl, we must have tea and discuss the most exciting news," the countess said, taking her hand, and leading her down the hallway toward the parlor. Once there she imperiously rang the bell, and a maid quickly appeared and received their order for tea and cakes.

"Upon my word, what is it, Mamma, you are all aflutter."

They made their way to the chaise longue by the windows which overlooked the gardens. In the distance, she made out the distinct form of Simon walking with another man. Her heart jerked, and memories of his wonderful kisses and touch brought a flush of heat to her cheeks. She quickly looked away and toward her mother, whose eyes sparkled with excitement.

"Not an hour ago, William James Astor, the twelfth Duke of Wycliffe arrived from India where he had been for the last six years! He will be under this very roof for the next few days, I'm told before he heads to Hampshire."

"I see," Miranda murmured, her heart sinking. "A duke is in residence."

"Yes," her mother crowed with delight. "And I heard him mention to Dr. Astor while they were ensconced in the library that he has returned to fulfill his duty, that he had been idle enough abroad."

Miranda was aghast. "Mamma, how could you eavesdrop on Dr. Astor and his guest?"

"The duke is Dr. Astor's brother. And he plans to marry by next season! This is a most fortuitous opportunity, my dear. How lucky we are to have been put up in this very household!"

A bubble of confusion rushed through Miranda. "His brother?" She sucked in a sharp breath. "Sim…Dr. Astor's brother is *here*?"

"Yes. I never knew the good doctor had such connections," her mother said with a pleased smile.

Dread lodged against Miranda's stomach like a

heavy stone at the glint of matrimonial fervor in her mother's eyes.

"I knew there must be a reason the good Lord allowed us to be stranded here. The duke returned inside a few minutes ago for a decanter of liquor and two glasses. Very odd at this time of the day but not overly improper," her mother said primly. "I contrived to run into him in the hallway and affect an introduction. How charming and unaffected he was with his manners and flattery. And terribly handsome as well. He is not current with his fashion, but that is to be expected being away for so long!"

Her mother clapped her hands together, fairly bubbling with her happiness. "This is the perfect opportunity to present yourself to the duke. Oh, Miranda, all our dreams can come true."

The raw, painful emotions tearing through her were wholly unexpected, and her silence could be suffered no longer. "To marry a duke is not my dream, Mamma," she said softly. "That is *yours*. I've not met this man, and yet you are here conspiring for us to wed! I have no wish to marry a duke, a prince, or a titled peer unless I *love* him, and he loves me in return."

And I know I am hopelessly falling in love with Simon Astor.

Miranda feared despite his connections he would never be thought an eligible husband for the daughter of an earl. The third son would not do when an eligible duke was available. The fervor of matrimonial fever had been lit inside her mother, her eyes glinted with mischief and, to Miranda's mind, villainous intent. Oh, she could not bear it if her mother were to try and force a connection between them. She might very well die of humiliation, rage, and heartache.

Her mother, father, and brother would be most violently opposed to the idea of a union between her and Dr. Astor. Mamma would do all that lay within her power to prevent her daughter from marrying a man whom she unequivocally disapproved. Even if it meant locking her away. Her thought felt morbid and overly morose.

The countess lowered the curtains and peered at her daughter. "Miranda, not this unreasonable obstinacy again. Affections will eventually come with the man you marry."

She took a steadying breath. "I've formed an attachment with Dr. Astor. I admire him most ardently and—"

"No!" her mother gasped in such a horrified tone, Miranda stopped speaking.

Her mother took her hands between hers. "My dear, while Dr. Astor's situation in life is respectable, he is *not* your equal in station and would make a marriage between you both quite ineligible by our family's standard. I trust you are neither so foolish nor so undutiful as to conduct yourself in a way that might encourage him to make an offer."

"Mamma I love him, and he has suitable connections—"

"Connections!" her mother snapped with icy disdain, releasing her hand. "You are not to marry a man who has connections, but a man who is of great rank and privilege, certain of his place and position in the *haut monde*. I shall hear no more of this nonsense with Dr. Astor!"

"And if he loves and respects me? Should that not be just as important as wealth and consequences. Do you not love papa?"

An expression of scandalized dismay settled on the countess's countenance. "Are these the discussions you've been having with the doctor?"

Miranda lifted her chin. "Our feelings are known to each other."

Her mother appeared faint. "I'll not hear

another word of this, young lady! I must summon Henry at once, perhaps he will be able to talk some much-needed good sense into you."

Miranda closed her eyes in frustration. "Mamma! If you will but for one moment consider *my* happiness in your plans," she said in a voice thick with tears. "For a moment, Mamma, think of what I desire. I will not be forced—"

A knock sounded, robbing her speech. Simon entered with his brother, and Miranda and her mother surged to their feet. Her eyes were for Simon, but a sharp inhalation of appreciation tugged her gaze to the man beside him.

The resemblance between the brothers was uncanny, except there was an air of hardness and insouciance about the duke. She thought she saw sadness and sorrow woven in the depths of his blue eyes.

Simon stepped forward. "Countess Langford, Lady Miranda, may I present my brother, William Astor, the Duke of Wycliffe. William, the countess, and her daughter have been my guests these last several days while the countess recovers from a bad sprain."

The duke bowed, "I'm charmed," he said, his eyes never leaving Miranda's person.

"And we are delighted," her mother said, dipping into a most graceful curtsy.

Miranda curtsied, and when she lifted her eyes, both brothers stared at her with similar, piercing regards. She realized she was quite fetching in a layered golden gown which clung to her slender frame, and her dark golden hair had been styled in a becoming chignon. Still, it was no cause for the duke who did not know her to stare so boldly.

Oddly, she could not read the emotions in Simon's eyes, for usually she would only spy tender regard in his gaze.

"I must take my leave, and unfortunately I will not be present at dinner this evening. Mrs. Chudleigh is in labor, and I must attend her in the village. Vicar Powell and his wife are my guests for dinner this evening. William, please convey my apologies as I must attend to my patient."

The offer to accompany him hovered on her tongue, but she bit it back before she scandalized her mother and the duke. But how badly she wished to assist him, and it gladdened her heart that he would not be the type of husband who would want to curtail her to household duties and balls and parties hosting.

"I shall take excellent care of your guests," the

duke said with a warm, inviting smile, to which Miranda did not respond.

His brow arched as if he was not accustomed to a lady resisting his charms. She almost rolled her eyes. Simon's lips twitched, and it was evident he fought back a smile.

"I will bid you ladies good evening." Then with a bow, he departed the parlor, responding to his call of duty.

"Should I call for tea, Your Grace?" her mother asked with an affable charm.

"I would like that."

"Lady Miranda's skill at the pianoforte is unsurpassed. Might she play for us while we wait for the teapot to be refreshed."

"I would like that," the duke said, walking to sit on the sofa closest to the pianoforte. "I...I knew someone once, and she loved music. I've not heard anyone play since."

And suddenly Miranda did not mind playing, for she sensed the duke loved and missed whoever he spoke of. She ambled over to the pianoforte and lifted the gleaming lid. Closing her eyes, she allowed her fingers to dance over the keys bringing rich, vibrant music alive. She started to sing, and she heard her mother's sigh of pleasure, and she wished

Simon had been present, for it was him she sang and played for.

Later that night, a knock sounded on Miranda's door, she closed the book she'd been reading, and glanced up. It was frightfully late, after midnight at least. And still, Simon had not returned. He had sent word that Mrs. Chudleigh's labor might very well continue into tomorrow and he would spend the night at her residence. A pulse of worry slithered through Miranda when a more strident knock sounded, and she pushed from the bed, tugging her robe from the peg and slipping it on. She hurried to the door and opened it, to see Agnes standing with a lantern, a fierce and worried frown on her face.

"Agnes, what is it, is it Mamma?"

"It is, milady, we must go to her room right away." She turned and moved with speed down the hallway.

Her heart tripping in alarm, Miranda followed. She frowned when Agnes went past the countess's door. "Is Mamma not in her room?"

There was a slight hitch in Agnes's step then she said, "Lady Langford most stringently complained of a draught in her room, and the housekeeper was obliged to move her, milady."

Miranda rolled her eyes in exasperation. Mamma had been such a tiring guest. She tried to feel some sympathy, for it could not be easy for a woman used to such activities as taking long walks and riding to be confined to her bed. Still, Mamma should handle the situation with more grace than she had done, and Miranda would tell her so. And they must repay Simon's goodwill with a charity fundraiser ball for his hospital. She would insist on it.

They came upon a door, and lamp light showed from behind the door. Mamma was clearly awake. Agnes knocked once, opened the door and held it wide for Miranda to enter. She proceeded inside and grounded to a halt to see the Duke of Wycliffe standing by the fire with a glass in his hand and dressed only in a banyan. He glanced up with a warm, welcoming smile, and Miranda's heart fluttered to her chest in sheer shock.

The door slammed shut, and she spun around with such speed for a moment she felt lightheaded. She rushed toward the door, only to hear the decisive turning of a key in the lock.

CHAPTER 9

"Agnes!" Miranda cried, horror icing through her veins. "Open this door at once! Please do not let Mamma convince you to do this!"

The sound of footsteps running away reached Miranda's ears, and she groaned her frustration and thumped the door. "Agnes!"

"Ahem," the duke said.

She whirled around and narrowed her eyes at him. "Do you by chance have a key to this chamber, Your Grace?"

A discomfited expression settled on his face and with a sigh, he stepped back. "I gather you did not send me a note mentioning you would slip into my room for a rendezvous?"

Miranda gasped, "I most certainly did not! I am a lady of good sense, Your Grace, I am barely acquainted with you."

Silence throbbed in the room like a wound.

The hint of seductive laughter had entirely vanished from his eyes. "I see." A calculating glint entered his eyes. "Either you are the greatest actress alive, or you are truly innocent in this farce."

"And I truly do not care a fig about what you think or believe! Do you have a key?" she asked through gritted teeth.

"Alas, I do not."

If she had to marry the duke…the thought was just too awful to contemplate. Frustrated tears burned behind her eyes. *How could you, Mamma?* Miranda hurried to the window and shoved it open, staring at the three-story fall. She glanced back at the four-poster bed, and the billowing curtains surrounding it. In the gothic novels she read, the heroine is always tying bedsheets and curtains together to escape some dastardly situation. Perhaps…

"It will not work, and I would be the worst sort of bounder to watch you act foolishly and fall to your death."

She whirled around, ashamed to feel tears springing to her eyes. "I cannot spend the night in your room, Your Grace."

Resignation settled on his face, and he raked his fingers through his dark hair. "I'm afraid the deed is already done, even if you were to be rescued now, your reputation is compromised. And I do not feel as if rescue would come until the morning. Is that not what your mother planned?"

Miranda winced, mortification crawling through her. "I cannot beg forgiveness for her actions, for I do not perceive I will be able to forgive her anytime soon. Mamma will expect for you to offer for me and—"

"Upon my honor, I will marry you."

She stared at him utterly aghast. "Your Grace, you cannot!" She didn't know whether to laugh or to weep. Finally, a duke willing to marry her, one who was quite handsome, wealthy, and respected. And she did not want him, instead she desired his brother with every emotion in her heart. She could no longer think of him as simply a diversion any longer or a passing flirtation. She had fallen in love with him. He was a man well worth wanting. Worth risking the wrath of her parents for. Worth denying a duke for. "I'll not marry you."

Her refusal genuinely seemed to astonish him. His arrogance and his lack of outrage ruffled her composure. He settled a palm against his chest. "I've decided to marry, and this compromising situation will simply push up my timeline for the deed. You are very comely, and Simon extols your grace, kindness, and intelligence. I daresay you will make me a fine duchess and will save me the horror of wading through the London season to find a match."

"Your Grace, you are quite mistaken on the matter. While I am sure you'll be the most eligible catch of the season, I am not at all interested in being your bride," she said bluntly. "And I never will be."

An arched brow winged. "Is this not what you want?"

"No, I have the utmost regard and tender sentiment for another and cannot bear the thought of marrying anyone but him!"

His harsh features softened unexpectedly. "And will he feel the same once it is known you spend the night in my room, dressed in such a revealing manner?"

At his provocatively infuriating words, she clutched the robe tighter to her throat. *I loved her, but she thought the wealth and stature of my brother would suit her better.*

Her throat went tight with emotions and doubt.

She took small retreating steps away from the duke, desperate to maintain a distance between them. "I'll sleep on the chaise longue, Your Grace."

"Nonsense, you'll take the bed."

"I'll not have, when that door conveniently opens in the morning, being found in your bed," she whispered furiously.

He sighed. "Lady Miranda, the damage has already been done. You are thoroughly compromised, and we must prepare to deal with the situation."

She was alarmed at the possibility that he was right. Too overwrought to cross words with him, she made her way to the chaise, settled atop the cushions, and closed her eyes. She tossed a few times, before she turned on her side, away from the duke. Silence lingered within the confines of the room, and she was appalled to feel tears coursing down her temple. Exhaustion pulled her into sleep, and as she drifted off, she felt the duke tucking a blanket about her waist.

. . .

Hours after he had been in Mrs. Chudleigh's home, Simon trudged up the winding staircase of his home, his exhaustion heavy. The labor had been burdensome to Mrs. Chudleigh, and he feared childbed fever setting in. She had been in a weakened state when he left, but fresh air circulated in her tiny room which he had ordered to be cleaned.

The squalling baby girl would need a wet nurse, for he believed Mrs. Chudleigh was too weak to attend the task herself. A humorless smile curved his mouth when he recalled his mother's distaste that he would study under a surgeon. She had thought it unrefined to a man of his standing, but without all those pieces of knowledge gleaned over the years from studying surgeons and midwives, Mrs. Chudleigh might have very well died tonight. Simon had tasked her husband to watch her for the night, for he had been concerned about the heat in her flesh. Laudanum would ease her sleep for the night, but she had to be carefully observed for signs of a fever or prolonged bleeding. He would snatch a few hours of rest and then ride out to see Mrs. Chudleigh and the baby again in the morning.

How he wished Miranda had been with him.

Somehow, he sensed her steady strength and unflinching bravery would have been a great assistance to him tonight. Upon reaching the landing, he shifted left, staring along the darkened hallway leading to her chamber.

A tug of need, to quietly sit with her, to see her face after such hours of grueling work dragged his feet to her chamber. No light shone from beneath her door, and he was quite aware it was about two in the morning. Lifting a hand, he knocked on her door, but no answer came. Scrubbing a hand over his face, Simon went into his chamber, thankful to see Mrs. Clayton had arranged for the bath to be filled before his arrival. The water was tepid, but he stirred and sank into the large copper tub, scrubbing the sweat and grime of the day away.

A few minutes later, he lay atop his pristine sheets, and closed his eyes, allowing the thoughts of Miranda to be the last thing to crowd his mind before he fell into a restful and much-needed slumber.

A FEW HOURS LATER, an overly dramatic gasp roused Miranda from sleep. Exhaustion still weighed on her lips, for she had only fallen into deep rest with the dawn but suffered uneasy dreams. She shifted on the chaise and sat up, glaring at the people framed in the doorway. Her mamma, Henry, the housekeeper Mrs. Clayton, Vicar Powell, and his wife, and shockingly, Mrs. Denniston. Miranda almost wept with relief that Simon was not amongst the witnesses her mother had gathered. Her mother affected the right tones of motherly shock and offended propriety when she demanded, "Upon my word! What is happening here?"

That screech roused the duke who had still been sleeping in his bed. To his credit, as he stood, he revealed he remained fully clothed, down to his polished boots.

Mrs. Powell's gasp of alarm echoed in the space and she paled alarmingly. "You…Your Grace," she stammered, appearing faint.

"This is an outrageous breach of conduct!" the Vicar blustered.

"Good God, man, what is the meaning of this?" Henry's demand rang with the shade of truth. His usually amiable countenance was stern with disapproval. Miranda supposed Mamma had not kept him abreast of her devious plans.

"My daughter has spent the night with his

Grace! Oh my, Miranda is ruined," her mother wailed. "Only immediate marriage may render her respectable."

The Vicar nodded with pompous authority. "Indeed, it is."

The duke stepped forward and bowed. "I am uncertain as to how we were locked in the room but let me assure you no impropriety happened behind these doors. Lady Miranda slept on the chaise, and I on the bed."

Her mother began to protest, "An explanation of what happened is not sufficient to render my daughter respectable. Your Grace—"

He smoothly interrupted. "My fiancée and I met briefly for a private discussion, and we got stuck together."

Her mother's hand fluttered to her throat. "Your fiancée?" she murmured, her eyes glittering with pleasure.

"We'd planned an announcement today," he said smoothly, playing the game deftly. "Of course, this awkward situation has caused us to reveal our attachment in this manner."

A collective sigh of relief went through the small gathering, for scandal had been averted and honor satisfied. Miranda observed the farce playing before her, and felt as if she were in a sea, drowning in uncertainty, trepidation, and pain. She ambled forward, straight at the cluster of people who parted at the very last minute. Without speaking to anyone, and too ashamed and infuriated to look at her mother, she walked away with her head held high to her room.

Her heart was breaking, for Miranda understood very well the power of gossips and how terribly damaging it would be to her reputation. The Vicar and his wife would be the first to inform their parishioners in discreet whispers of the scandalous tryst they had witnessed. Then it would spread like wildfire through the country and then onto London and the ballrooms and newssheets.

She *was* ruined, and only marriage to the duke would be deemed a satisfactory outcome.

You've won, Mamma.

Miranda closed the door to her room, and slowly slid against it until her bottom touched the floor. She tugged her knees up and pressed her forehead against them. "Oh Simon," she whispered, her voice breaking, and tears coursing down her cheeks. And for a long time, she stayed there, crying, ignoring all the knocks and concerned murmurs at her door, for she feared she had lost the only chance of happiness she might have had with the man she loved.

CHAPTER 10

An odd air of expectation blanketed the breakfast room this morning, and Simon assessed his guests with a decidedly critical eye. The Vicar had spent two minutes discussing the sins of the flesh and how wickedly immoral it is to cave in to temptation before marriage. For a wild moment, he had wondered if the man had peered into his heart and soused the passion he had brewing for Miranda. Then he noted the tension in her shoulders and the pain in her eyes. That pain affected him, and as soon as everyone had dispersed, he would take her on their walk and find out what had happened. He sat there hoping she would smile or glance in his direction, but she stared straight ahead, an air of melancholy surrounding her.

"We have an announcement to make," the countess said with a bright smile.

"Oh?" Henry said, glancing from Miranda to the duke. Yet Simon sensed he very knew well what his mother was about.

Simon frowned, lowering his fork even as his brother sighed with resignation and an emotion he could not place.

"Are you leaving, my lady?" Though he dearly hoped not. He wanted more time with Miranda, for Simon was sure he wanted to marry her, and he needed a bit of time with the countess before he visited her father. He wasn't confident he could wait for next season to start a courtship. Nor did he want to risk some other gentleman with all the right consequences stealing away her affections. Though on that score he did not indeed worry, she did not have an inconstant heart, and he felt in every touch, kiss, and smile she gave him that she too was falling in love.

The awareness clutched fiercely at his heart, and he smiled at her. Her lower lip trembled before she firmed her mouth. Yet she did not return his smile.

"His Grace, your brother, offered for Miranda, and I have accepted on her behalf," the countess said with a wide smile. "Of course, given the delicate circumstances, a quick wedding would be most prudent."

The words were like a solid blow to the center of Simon's chest. For a terrible, timeless minute, he could do nothing but stare at the countess. An unexpectedly strange weakness assailed him. It took such strength at that moment to lift his head and examine Miranda's features. Her expression was coolly composed, her eyes blank, but her lips formed no denial. Simon's heart twisted into painful knots, then it cracked, and his chest damn well ached.

Simon shifted his regard to his brother. "Is this true?" he demanded hoarsely.

His brother frowned and lowered his eyes to the knife gripped in Simon's hand. Knowledge seeped into William's eyes, and a pained regret glowed there. "I...yes. I was honor bound to."

Simon flinched, understanding so much from that simple statement. There had been a compromising situation, and nothing was more important to his brother than honor and duty. Whatever the situation had been, William's honor would have prompted him to marry her, and it was merely his luck that she was a charming beauty, with a quick intelligence, and from a prominent, well connected, and respectable family.

"I am quite pleased with the alliance, and I've written to the earl this morning of the happy news. He'll ensure notices are posted to the papers."

The pain that pierced his heart was numbing. Her mother was not inclined to tarry at all, and he could see the jubilation in her eyes.

"I see."

"Excellent news all around," the vicar said. "We understand you've just returned from abroad, and to find a bride so soon. Excellent news indeed, and you have mine and Mrs. Powell's heartiest congratulations. And you may rest assured of our discretion, Your Grace. We shall not mention that the lady spent the entire night in your room to anyone at all. I am sure it was all above board as you've assured us."

Their gazes collided and tears burned in her eyes. And now he understood why she had not been in her room last night. The heaviness in his heart was an unbearable weight. And he sensed with every breath in his body it had not been done by her design.

Miranda's chair pushed back abruptly. "If you'll excuse me, I have to oversee the packing of my valise, and I am without appetite."

Then she hurried from the room as if devils chased her.

Mrs. Clayton rushed inside and said, "Beg pardon, Dr. Astor, a boy from the Chudleighs' is here. The boy is a crying mess."

He wanted nothing more than to chase Miranda and figure a way out of her mother's calculating mess. But from the grave look in Mrs. Clayton's eyes, he knew it was severe. He glanced at his brother and the rest of his guests. "If you'll excuse me, my patient is in dire need of me. I must leave immediately." He sketched a short bow and spun around.

"Dr. Astor, are you not to offer your brother congratulation on a most fortuitous match?"

The countess's words arrested his movement briefly, but he did not dignify the smugness of her question with a response. He walked away, ignoring her gasp of affront.

He had a patient to save, and he could not abide the dark pain scraping at his insides. His housekeeper had his medical bag waiting for him in the hallway.

"Your horse has been saddled, Doctor."

"Thank you, Mrs. Clayton," he said, hurrying through the front door and to the stable hand who waited with his horse.

The ride to the Chudleighs was more than half an hour, and he felt keen regret he had not been able to convince her husband that her last days of confinement should be done at Riversend Manor. When he arrived, he was quickly ushered inside their bedroom, to find a delirious Mrs. Chudleigh.

"Cool water from the well, immediately," he ordered, taking off his jacket and rolling his sleeves. He had a few herbs in his bag which had been noted by several medical journals to reduce fever when boiled and consumed.

"Has she eaten or drunk anything?"

"Just a bit of bare water," Mr. Jeremy Chudleigh said, his grey eyes dark with worry. "We've had two boys before, and she never got like this after."

"The labor was especially draining," Simon replied. "But she is a strong woman, do not lose heart."

The man nodded, grateful for the encouraging words.

Simon dipped into his bag and took out a small sac with roots. He broke off a piece and handed it to Jeremey. "Boil this in some water, and then when it is cool bring it to me."

Her oldest boy, a lad of ten years hurried back with the basin of cold water and a towel.

"Bring me two more jugs," he told the boy. "And more fresh linens."

Simon washed his hands, shooed them from the room, then lifted the sheets draped over Mrs. Chudleigh's lower body and examined her. The bleeding had slowed which was a good sign, but she burned with a worrying fever. He stayed for hours, sponging her down in cool water, and forcing broth and the juice from the boiled root down her throat. Simon never left her side, and by the time her fever broke, dusk had fallen, and the sun had vanished leaving a pale moonlight hovering in the sky.

Mr. Chudleigh cried when he got the news his wife was well, and Simon spent several minutes informing him of how long he should abstain from sexual activities and a few acceptable methods to prevent pregnancy. He would not recommend Mrs. Chudleigh falling with child again.

Jeremy had agreed and had given him a humble offer of bread and an apple which Simon devoured. Now he made his way home, and as he crossed the threshold, an unknown instinct warned him that Miranda was no longer there.

Mrs. Clayton ambled toward him, a questioning look in her eyes.

"Mrs. Chudleigh is she—"

"She will recover quite well."

Relief lit in her eyes. "I shall pay a visit to her tomorrow."

"And I would appreciate it if you could take a few baskets of groceries with you. Whatever you can find in the larder. Meat from the butcher as well and send the bill to me. And whatever we have in the vegetable gardens."

"Yes, Dr. Astor."

She turned and drifted down the hall, and though he hated to ask, he said, "Mrs. Clayton… Lady Miranda."

"She left, Dr. Astor…with her mother and brother some few hours ago. I believe they've headed on to Lincolnshire."

"Did she…leave any message or note?"

"She did not, Sir."

"Thank you, Mrs. Clayton." He cleared his throat. "Good night."

He made his way to his chamber but could not find sleep. Simon stood at the soaring windows of his room which overlooked the vast expanse of his estate. He stayed there, his eyes dry, and an unfathomable pain in his heart, until the sun crested and broke in the sky.

Simon could not sleep or eat without dreaming of Miranda. She, her mother, and brother had departed his home only three days past, and he was already tormented with missing her. The news of an engagement between the pair had already been printed in the newspapers, and his district was agog with the story.

He tried to bury himself in work, which did little to distract him for all his patients had been sent home. Mrs. Chudleigh and the baby were quite excellent, and he only did one house call this morning to the Squire who was now hobbling around on crutches. Reading his numerous medical journals did not distract his mind, and his heart was a continual aching mess.

Years ago when he had fancied himself in love with Miss Phoebe Cranston, she had climbed into his brother's bed in hopes of landing a duke. The pain from that betrayal had lasted a few hours before he had hardened his heart against feeling any emotions for a lady who had not regarded him with similar sentiments.

Simon desperately tried to draw on that similar reserve to dull the pain of losing Miranda and could not find it anywhere. With a snarl of frustration, he slammed the medical tome closed, stood, and prowled over to the windows overlooking the lake. It would be unbearable knowing how much he loved her and seeing her at his brother's side as his duchess.

There had been a look in her eyes when she had fled the breakfast parlor a few days ago. It had been one of rank disappointment, mortification, and pain. Was it that he had dashed her expectations by remaining silent? Should he have declared to all that he loved her and would not allow his brother, the duke, to marry her? How laughable that would be. Her father would not consent for them to marry when he had a duke in his back pocket, one who was eager to wed a delectable beauty such as Miranda. And even if William knew Simon was desperately in love with her, his honor would not allow him to cry off.

It had been announced in the papers. A greater scandal would ensue if William were to call off their engagement, and her reputation would be in shambles. Though he was aware of all this, it felt entirely too bleak to contemplate living the rest of his days without Miranda.

Echoing footsteps sounded behind him. "A letter arrived for you, Dr. Astor. It is from the duchess."

His mother had heard the news then. "Thank you, Mrs. Clayton."

He opened the letter and read.

Dear Simon,

Please attend to us at dinner at Hawthorne Park this Sunday. My dear William has been engaged to one of the loveliest girls of the season, from a perfect and respectable family. I'd not thought my heart could be more overjoyed to have him return home with us. But a wedding, and perhaps a grandchild to dote on very soon has filled me with such hope and happiness.

I miss you dreadfully, my dear boy, and I hope to see you soon. Lady Miranda and her family will also dine with us as we gather to celebrate William and Lady Miranda's fortuitous attachment.

Your loving mother, Amelia, the Duchess of Wycliffe.

Another chance to see her again. He had always

been so decisive choosing his path in life, so certain of his purpose in all he did, yet now he felt adrift, uncertain of his next steps forward. He believed in never wasting one of the most precious things about humanity—time. It waited on no man, and as a physician, he had seen many regret not having fought for what they had wanted from life. Even in William, he saw the keen regret he had not eloped with Sophia and ignored their parents' objection to their marriage.

Miranda aroused Simon's mind, body, and soul, and he did not want a future without her in it. Simon was certain as the rising sun that he could not allow Miranda to slip from his life. Perhaps if he had thought her happy with being William's wife he could have stepped back. For she deserved love, to be cosseted, and treasured. William had no heart or tender sentiments to offer her, for he had buried those along with Sophia.

And even in that, Simon lied to himself. No more, he silently snapped. He rubbed a hand against his chest at the pain that pierced him at the thought of Miranda in his brother's arms, her eyes deadened by his eventual indifference.

He had the sudden, inexplicable feeling that he did not truly know the full heart and character of the woman he loved, and he had a lifetime with her ahead of him to learn her layers, if only he would but reach and fight for her.

Turning around, he faltered to see Mrs. Clayton hovering in the doorway. "It is a request for me to attend a dinner with William…and Lady Miranda and her family."

"Will you go?"

"Yes."

She hesitated then said, "Pardon the impertinence, Dr. Astor, will you let her slip away from you?"

"No."

His housekeeper smiled. "Good, for I've never seen you so completed before, Sir." Then she turned away. "I'll arrange for your departure, Doctor."

And though he did not know what he would say, Simon said, "I want to leave at first light."

CHAPTER 11

The Cheswick family had been summoned to Hawthorne Park, the ancestral seat of the Duke of Wycliffe, and that of her fiancé. Over the last few days Miranda had felt numbed with a sense of betrayal and such hurt she had been unable to sleep, nor had she been able to speak to her mother despite the countess's overtures. How she had missed him and feared she had disgusted him. Simon had been so silently furious in his condemnation, yet he had not spoken out against the engagement. *Why not? Why have you given up so easily…did you not love me?*

She had eventually closed her heart against the recriminations, understanding there was nothing he could have done. Her mother had contrived for the duke and her to be in a locked room overnight, and her reputation was soiled. It mattered little that only the occupants of Riversend Manor, the duke, and the vicar and his wife, were aware of the scandalous situation, her mother would demand her pound of flesh, and the duke seemed to breathe honor.

They had only been at Seaview Park, their country home for a few hours before they received a letter from the duchess inviting them to dinner. And the following morning, another arduous journey had begun as they made their way to Hampshire via carriage.

Mira remained silent for the several days' journey, with her nose buried inside a book. They stayed overnight at some respectable inns along the way, and at night when alone, she cried into her pillows until sleep claimed her. When each day she rose to continue the journey her mother would stare at her puffed up eyes, but no comment was asked for, and she did not render an explanation.

The ache in her chest became a physical thing, and there was no ease in its tightening grip. It had been a little over a week, and whenever she envisioned a life beside the duke, being his wife, hosting his dinners and political parties, sharing his kisses and bed, she became numb. That was a life she could not bear to tolerate for herself, and Miranda knew she could not do it.

They arrived at Hawthorne Park, and her mother gasped, "Look at what you will be mistress of!"

And though it was one of the most beautiful estates she had ever seen, with a large stately home which boasted more than one hundred rooms, she remained unmoved. The Duchess and William greeted Miranda, her parents, and her brother, and they went into a lavishly furnished drawing room for tea.

The Duchess was still quite beautiful, and Miranda supposed she had not yet reached fifty. She was dressed in lavender silk trimmed with black ribbon bows, which denoted half mourning although her husband had been dead for more than six years. On one of their long walks, Simon had explained she had slipped into deep melancholia for she had loved him very much.

To Miranda's mind, the entire scene had been filled with tension, for despite trying, she could manage no more than a one-word reply to each of the duchess's probing questions. Propriety and gratitude for her acceptance as her son's future wife, dictated that Miranda should be utterly polite and eager to gain the duchess's approval, but she could not find the energy to care.

"I am terribly sorry. The journey has been tiring, and I would like to rest before dinner."

"Of course, my dear," the duchess said, her blue eyes sharp and questioning.

Her papa, whose only interest in the visit was that he might do a spot of fishing during his weeklong visit to Hawthorne Park sent her a probing look of concern which she returned with a wan smile. Miranda had not told him of Mamma's conduct, already knowing he would do whatever his wife wanted. He had always weakly obeyed her strictures throughout the years and the meekness of his character Miranda believed her mamma shamelessly took advantage of.

Miranda was excused, and she got some rest before Agnes roused her to be dressed.

"Milady, please forgive me," Agnes said, tears filling her eyes. "I've never seen you so unhappy, and I feel wretched to have been a party to your pain."

Miranda sighed. "Pray do not regard it, Agnes. If you had objected or refused my mother, I daresay you would have been dismissed without references. I shall be quite fine."

She gave her a reassuring smile and allowed Agnes to dress her in one of the most ravishing gowns she owned. Her mother had insisted upon the dark rose low cut gown with its tightly cinched waist and narrow skirt. It flattered her figure most becomingly. Her hair was caught up in a riot of curls with a few artful tendrils kissing her cheeks. When she saw herself in the mirror, Miranda was pleased with her appearance. No one had to know that inside she was ravaged and bleeding.

Promptly at eight, she descended the stairs and was guided by a footman to a large and elegantly appointed drawing room. The duke surged to his feet at her entrance and admiration lit his eyes.

"You are a delight to behold, Lady Miranda," he murmured.

She offered him a tight smile, unable to speak beyond the emotions in her throat. As propriety dictated, he led his mother inside the dining room, her papa escorted her mother, and Henry accompanied Miranda.

"Simon!" the duchess gasped.

Miranda stiffened as she saw him already seated. Her knees weakened, and she clutched at Henry's arm. He sent her a swift, concerned glance but she could not wrest her gaze from Simon. He looked wonderful, dressed in dark jacket and trousers, with a white shirt and a blue waistcoat. His hair was well groomed, and his cravat was tied expertly. She had never seen him more handsome and coolly aloof.

He stood and bowed. "I took the liberty of waiting in here for you to arrive, Mamma."

"Why wasn't I informed you had arrived, my boy?" she hurried over to him and clasped him in a fierce embrace.

"I confess I designed it that way," he said with a small smile at his mother.

Over her head, their gazes collided and the warmth in his stole her breath. She sent him a tremulous smile, while her heart pounded a breathless rhythm. Soon they were all seated, and the courses of watercress soup, game pie, lamb cutlets, mushroom fritters, roast beef, baked pike, artichoke hearts followed by rose water-flavored ice, jellies in a flower shape, fruit compote, and Genoese cake were served. Dinner was quite animated, though Miranda had little to say. Almost two hours had passed before the duchess ordered champagne to be served. Once the footmen had their glasses filled, she beamed at everyone.

"I cannot adequately express my happiness that

my son is getting married, and to such a lovely girl, despite her being a little timid."

A few strained chuckles went around the table, and her mother sent her a glance which promised a fierce scolding.

"I would like to make a toast…." She smiled at Simon who had stood and lifted his glass. "Though I gather your younger brother is eager to go first."

Miranda's heart thumped as he stared at her, and she nervously glanced around the table.

"I am not a man of many words, and I hope the few that I have will convey my feelings." He cleared his throat and glanced at his brother. "I know your honor is very important to you, but I must explain that Lady Miranda is my Sophia."

The duchess gasped and lowered her glass onto the table with an audible thud. "Simon?" she questioned sharply.

William stared at his brother, an expression of shock on his face. Simon shifted to face her. "I love you," he merely said.

"What is this?" her father demanded, pushing back his chair and standing. "I demand an explanation."

"I love your daughter, Lord Langford, and I

believe she loves me as well. A union between her and my brother would be a mistake, for he does not love her, nor does she love him. Your countess conspired for them to be compromised, and then my brother merrily went along with her conniving because he wants a wife without the messy emotion of love."

Her father breathed deeply. "Nonetheless, an offer has been made, our family has accepted, and the engagement has been posted! There will be no scandal," he roared.

A painful silence fell over the room, yet Simon did not take his eyes from hers.

"I am not entirely sure what will happen from here," he said hoarsely. "But I am supposing we should run away."

The duchess looked ready to faint, and Miranda's mother squawked her outrage.

"We cannot," Miranda whispered, "The scandal would be too dreadful…"

He flinched, and she wanted to scream at the pain which darkened his gaze. He lowered his hand, sketched a bow, turned and walked away.

"My very first memory was my mamma telling me how beautiful I am…and that one day I would marry a prince," her words though softly spoken had arrested everyone's attention, including Simon who had almost reached the door.

Miranda pushed back her chair and stood. The pain carved in his face almost made her weep. She pressed her hands into the table to prevent their visible trembling.

"If not a prince…only a duke would do. This man I was to marry would not care about my likes or dislikes, or my dreams and fears. The only thing of importance was that he would be well pleased with my beauty…and I would be contented with his perfect title, his lands, and his wealth. I asked her what if we did not like each other?" she glanced around the table, noting her mother's growing horror, the duchess's curious look, and her father's narrowed eyes. The duke himself had a frown on his face as he glanced between her and Simon.

"For many years I longed for this marriage…for my prince…and I've found him. His name is Simon Astor. I love him with my entire heart, and he loves the woman I am, with all my willful stubbornness, odd notions, for he sees beyond my beauty. He sees *me*…and loves all parts of me."

The duchess's jaw slackened, and she sat up straighter in her chair.

Her mother gazed at her as if she was a frightful

creature. "You wretched, ungrateful child," her mother sobbed.

"I will not be pressured into a marriage with a man whom I do not love."

"The engagement has been announced!" her mother cried. "The scandal—"

"I do not care about the scandal," she said, moving from around the table and slowly walking toward Simon. "I care about the man I love, living my life with him. You tried to take my choice from me, Mamma, and without a care of my happiness. You beseech me to wed a man I have no regards for in vain, for I will not succumb to such a life. We do not need to run away, my love. I am proudly choosing to walk by your side. I am of age to consent to marry you. While my parents' acceptance would be lovely…I…we, do not need it."

He drew her into his arms and hugged her. With a choked sob she returned his fierce embrace. Acute awareness of his hands resting against her back, the far-too-intimate nature of their embrace slithered through her. Then he kissed her, deeply, uncaring their families looked on.

Distantly she heard her father comforting her weeping mother, but Miranda hardly cared.

"Marry me," he murmured against her lips.

"Yes," she said laughing, and raining kisses over his face.

"This behavior is totally unseemly!" her mother wailed.

"Let's go," Simon murmured.

And trusting him, she slipped her hand in his and walked toward their future.

Thank you for reading **A Prince of my Own**!

I hope you enjoyed the journey to happy ever after for Miranda & Simon. **Reviews are Gold to Authors,** for they are a very important part of reaching readers, and I do hope you will consider leaving an honest review on Amazon adding to my rainbow. It does not have to be lengthy, a simple sentence or two will do. Just know that I will appreciate your efforts sincerely.

Continue reading for a sneak peek into the next book of the series

SOPHIA AND THE DUKE
Forever Yours Series Book 7
Excerpt

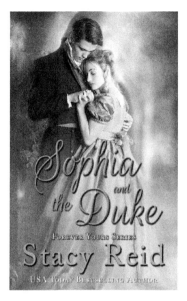

Grab a Copy Today

LADY MIRANDA CHESWICK IS BEAUTIFUL, witty, intelligent, and the family's great expectations are fAfter losing the family she loved, Miss Sophia Knightly lives a carefree and unrestricted life; her tomorrows are promised to no one. The last thing she expected was William Astor, the Duke of Wycliffe, to create the scandal of the Season by chasing after her at a ball.

William is the most compelling and sensual man Sophia has ever known, but she is not interested in resuming their kisses, guileless conversations, or his promises of forever. The duke, however, has other ideas…

William has vowed to have no other woman than Sophia Knightly and is willing to do whatever it takes to possess her. It started with a kiss, then a wicked invitation, and now there is no going back.

Soon the walls around Sophia's heart are crumbling . . . and she realizes the greatest adventure might be right in front of her!

CHAPTER ONE

Six years and eleven months later…

"*Marry me.*"
"*Yes.*"

It had been a little over an hour since his brother, Dr. Simon Astor, had walked away from Hawthorne Park's overly large dining room with William's fiancée in tow. Their mother, the duchess of Wycliffe, was still busy soothing the hysterical Countess Langford, who lamented loudly that Lady

Miranda, her daughter, had brought their entire family and reputation to ruin.

William chuckled mirthlessly, refilling his glass with whisky and tipping it to his lips. The person who had brought the Cheswick family's name into question was the countess herself, who had connived to compromise William with her daughter a few weeks previously, simply because he was the 12th duke of Wycliffe.

William had gone along with the farce because he knew he needed to acquire a wife. In a few weeks, he would be thirty, and the years he had spent abroad had filled his pockets with great wealth, but his heart remained an empty husk. His duty to the title was not one he would ever neglect, but he had thought it his obligation to finally return home from India and to seek a bride to marry. The farcical affair of Lady Miranda being trapped in his chamber under his brother's roof should have rescued William from wading through the *ton* to select a suitable future duchess. It had appeared to him at the time an easy decision to acquiesce to. The fact that Lady Miranda was also an acclaimed beauty, together with being the daughter of an earl had made her seem a perfectly acceptable bride. William had believed himself very fortunate with the turn of events until his brother Simon had spoken up.

"I know your honor is very important to you, but I must explain that Lady Miranda is my Sophia."

William rubbed the aching center of his chest that had burned to life upon Simon's words. If William had known that his brother loved Lady Miranda, he would never have made the offer. He lifted his glass in a toast to the eloping couple, admiring their audacity and bravery in the face of their family's and society's expectations.

A knock sounded on the door of the library. "Enter."

The scent of his mother's lavender perfume preceded her inside. He turned from the windows and observed her progress within the lavish space. His mother was dressed in the height of fashion, even if she yet wore half-mourning. Her lavender silk dress was pin-tucked decoratively into her still tiny waist. Its full sleeves tightening into delicate black lace cuffs. The neckline and hem of the full skirts ornamented with black lace, trimmed with opulent black ribbon bows. Mourning she had defiantly worn since her husband had died more than six years earlier from a failure of his heart. William thought his mother would have continued to wear black if she had thought the color suited her, but she looked very good in grays and shades of muted purple. A color she considered most suitable for a dowager duchess. His mother made her way to the mantle and to his amusement poured herself a healthy draft of whisky. The duchess took several swallows, spluttering slightly.

"The scandal will be absolutely dreadful," she said. "Whatever was your brother thinking! The countess is still totally prostrate with grief at their selfish actions. She is so disappointed that Miranda will not be your bride and dreads facing the embarrassment that will ensue. We must do everything within our power to stem the tide of scandal!"

"The countess was abominably selfish in trying to force her daughter to marry a man she does not love. I was just as damnably foolish to go along with her plan when I merely found Miranda attractive. I was wrong to think only that it would simplify my life and avoid a tedious search to find a wife. I regret the upset caused but I cannot regret standing aside for Simon and Miranda's happiness. Simon and the lady were true to their hearts. I will do my duty and find another bride."

His mother turned an appalled gaze in his

direction. "You sound as if you admire their outrageous conduct!"

William smiled briefly. "I do." Once many years ago he, William had thought about running away with the girl he'd loved more than duty and honor. He had lost her and it still hurt him deeply. If only he hadn't dawdled, seeking to persuade his parents to allow their marriage, their lives now would be of rich and contented fulfillment together. Instead, she was bones lying somewhere in a cold, unmarked grave. "I shall use all my influence to allow them to escape any scandal."

"The countess has already sent notices to the paper of your engagement to Miranda. Now the world will know you've been jilted."

"I'll admit to being such an ogre that the fair lady could not bear to endure my company for another minute."

His mother frowned. "That will not do. Your reputation must not bear any scrutiny—"

"I am certain it will not break," he said flatly and with considerable arrogance. "I *am* the duke of Wycliffe."

"How unconcerned you are," she huffed, taking another tentative sip of her drink. "I am sure you'll be running off to town for your share of amusements, and then you'll be at the nasty end of tonight's disaster. Though I must warn you there will not be much to be done now that the Season is ending," his mother said, watching him keenly.

William made a noncommittal sound, almost alarmed at the lack of interest he felt in the excitement and amusements of the *ton*. His mind and heart were stuck remembering the burning love which had glowed in Lady Miranda's eyes for his brother, and the mistake he had almost made in intending to rob them of that happiness. "There will be enough for me to do," he said, "And I'll be assuming my duties in the House of Lords at its next opening, and so now is a good time to reacquaint myself with the lords and ladies of the *ton*."

"And you'll be doing it amidst a brewing scandal!" she cried, her voice rich with displeasure. "Lady Miranda was perfect for you! So beautiful and poised."

But far more perfect for Simon.

An irritated sigh heaved from her. "I'll have to make a list of the eligible ladies for your perusal, and perhaps plan a garden party so you can meet as many as possible. I do believe Lady Vivian, the Earl of Granville's daughter, would be absolutely perfect for you!"

William considered his mother and the smile of strain about her lips. "I thought you would prefer to make your way to Bath to see your friend as soon as possible."

Her eyes widened, and she took several sips as if to gather her composure. "You know of the viscount?"

"Simon kept me abreast of happenings at home," he said, casually admitting to his knowledge of her affair with a man ten years younger than herself.

"I believed you would have been violently opposed to the idea, William."

"I have been away for years, Mother. Who am I to oppose any desire you have in your heart?"

She glanced away briefly before leveling her gaze on him once more. "You are the duke, the head of this family. You have at last taken up the duties and responsibilities of your station in life, it was always your destiny to be the duke and take your proper place in society. Now is the time when all propriety must be observed so the family name remains unblemished."

William took a long swallow of his whisky. "Are you happy, Mother? Does he make you happy?"

"Whenever I am in Bath...my joy is indescribable," she murmured, a flush mounting on her elegantly slanted cheekbones.

His mother was quite a handsome woman at eight and forty, with no hint of greying hair or wrinkles marring her exquisite face. In her youth she had been considered to outshine all the other debutantes and her hand had been avidly sought by the handsome young men of the *ton*. His father had been several years older but she had loved him openly and ardently. William knew how greatly she had been crushed by his father's death. How long she had grieved. Sorrow clutched at William's heart as he recalled how he had not been there to support her through her mourning. He had fled England's shore only months after his father's passing because he too had lost the love of his life and had found it difficult to remain where every sight, scent, taste, and even the rain reminded him of his Sophia.

Now his mother had healed from the loss of his father, how could he object to her affair. "You've decided to stop mourning?" he asked softly.

"Unexpectedly a few months ago I realized how alone I've been, and that I've hardly visited town and Bath. I've ordered a new wardrobe. Bright colors," she said with a wobbly smile.

"Do you wish to marry the viscount?"

She inhaled a sharp breath, her hand fluttering delicately to her throat. "Marry him?"

This was asked with such alarm he could see the thought had never entered her mind. "There is no need to say more, Mother, only know that you have our blessings if you wish to marry Viscount Bunbury."

The Viscount was a man of solid character according to Simon who'd gone to the trouble of investigating him. The viscount also had a good reputation in the *ton* and had his fortune. Despite the difference in their ages, the man seemed to genuinely want to be with his mother.

She stared at him for several moments before walking over and enfolding him in a hug. William wrapped his arms around her, carefully holding the glass of whisky away.

"Though you wrote to me often, I've missed you excessively, and I am very glad you are home," she murmured. Then with another squeeze of her arms, she released him and stepped away. "You've never really explored town and its attractions. I'll stay with you until a suitable—"

"Mother, please, return to Bath," he gently insisted.

"You have been away for so long. Surely you will need my help to navigate the waters of the *ton* and—"

He took her hands between his and smiled down at her. "Mother, I shall be fine. I am experienced enough to know what I desire in my wife."

The duchess thought of this for several minutes. "Very well."

He pressed a brief kiss to her cheek and then went over to the sideboard and refilled his glass with whisky. "I will make arrangements to travel to London immediately. No one will be aware that lady Miranda and I are no longer engaged until I enter the marriage mart. I am quite certain they will not announce to anyone that they've eloped."

The duchess nodded. "I will implore you, William, to recall your oath to your father that you would not marry a lady of inferior rank, fortune, and connections."

The glass being lifted to his lips stilled as if controlled by an external force. He stared at his mother, an odd pain twisting through him and piercing the numbness which he had carried for so long.

"I am now a man of nine and twenty," he murmured. "I made that oath to father years ago before he died." Only a few weeks after he'd lost Sophia and all the hopes he'd possessed for their future.

His mother's face took on a mutinous cast. "And you must be bound by it. To honor his memory. Your father, even in his illness, only wished to protect the family's reputation because you wanted to throw it away for that girl and—"

"Enough," he said with cutting precision. "I still recall with perfect clarity your objections to a girl I adored. I am no longer guided by sentiments or matters of the heart, so I assure you, madam, I will select the future duchess of Wycliffe while keeping in my mind my position and circumstances."

"And your promise to your father," she insisted stubbornly.

With a silent curse, he noted the strain across her lips and recalled to mind that Simon had mentioned hearing an odd beat of her heart when he had examined her for melancholia. The very idea of losing his mother to any serious illness or driving her to her sickbed with his remarks tempered him as nothing else could.

"I shall bear my duty in mind, Mama," he murmured, lifting her hand to his lip and kissing it. "And my promise to my father."

Some of the tension eased from her shoulders.

"And promise me, William," she said fiercely, "Promise me the wife you choose will be a young lady of quality whom I can approve and will be happy to call daughter, and her family my own."

His mother was never one to lose the opportunity to sink her claws home once she sensed weakness. It would not be an awkward thing to promise, for he had no notion of seeking an alliance based on tender feelings. This would be a marriage, one of mutual convenience, respect, and honor to each other. William truly did not care if he ever grew to love his wife or not, nor did he overly examine his apathy to tender sentiments. To his way of thinking, this could be achieved with any lady from the *ton*, from a respectable family.

"I promise it," he said, frowning at the cold arrow of discomfort that traveled through him at the vow.

What if…

With an inward snarl, he rejected the very

notion. He'd loved already and had lost her. To do so again he could not bear it. There would be no what if…only the simple transactions of a marriage contract to a young lady suitable to be his duchess. As he finished his conversation with his mother and made his way up the magnificent stairs to his chamber, he couldn't stop the insidious thought which curled through his heart.

What if…

Meanwhile in Hertfordshire…

Sophia laughed as she rounded the corner of the lanes at breakneck speed, urging her horse to the finish line. She tugged on the reins and slowed her chestnut mare, grinning as young Tommy, Lord Portman, halted his horse, too.

"You cheated," he accused, glaring at her. "Before I reached three, you darted away like a wild thing!"

"You've impugned my honor, dare I not demand a measure of satisfaction, my lord?" she asked with a wink.

Tommy chuckled at her deliberate impudence. "There is no hope for you, my dear Sophia, and it is no wonder mother despairs of finding you a husband."

Sophia sobered and glanced in the direction of the beautiful estate perched on the hill in the distance. "We all know the reason I've not made a match has nothing to do with—"

"Your hoydenish and unenthusiastic manners?" he said, repeating a refrain made by his mother, the countess Cadenham, over the years. "You challenged me to a race and then appeared in trousers! You will have to use the servants' entrance and sneak to your chamber lest Mama sees you."

"I daresay my lack of finding a husband has more to do with my lack of connections, fortune, and family than any of my escapades," she said with a heavy sigh, lifting her face to the last rays of the lowering sun.

He flinched, and shame rushed through her. "Tommy forgive me! I never meant to imply that you are not family."

"I know," he said after a few beats. "I own we will never be able to replace what you lost, Sophia."

She was unable to speak past the knot of emotions, tightening her throat. The acute memory of all that had been lost to her always filled her with overwhelming emotions. Several years ago, a disease epidemic had ravaged the sleepy and idyllic village of Mulford and had taken her mother, sister, and father in one cruel, heartrending blow. Somehow, Sophia had survived the illness after days of battling the fever, pain, and delirium. How she had screamed and torn at her hair when the doctor had informed her of the loss of her family. Still weakened she had fainted, and upon waking she had been in a carriage with her cousins, Lydia and Tommy, and her Aunt Imogen hovering over her. They had taken her away from Mulford and the unbearably weight of all that happened there.

All the happiness had been drained from Sophia's heart, and she'd only known bleakness for an exceedingly long time. It had taken several weeks to fully recover, and as soon as she had been able, Sophia had made her way back to Mulford. The memory of trekking for miles to Hardwick Park to the man she'd loved with her soul and being turned away stabbed the pain deeper into her heart, flaming it into agony.

"I did not mean to cast you into a somber mood," the viscount said.

She pushed away the memories and buried the

emotions deep under the surface of her heart. "Please do not regard it, Tommy, I am quite fine," she said with a smile that trembled on her lips.

"Will you travel to town tomorrow? Lady Pemberley's ball is one my sister is determined not to miss. I know you are not the sort to like these events, but Lydia is keen on attending, and without you to chaperone her, Mama will find it exhausting to sustain her attendance."

Lydia was Sophia's dearest friend and Tommy's twin sister. She suspected he wanted to pursue his own amusements elsewhere and did not want the trouble of escorting his sister to the ball. For the last few Seasons, the duty to be her cousin's companion and chaperone had fallen to her shoulders, and she hadn't protested, owing much to her aunt for taking her in without fuss or questions after the tragedy. Sophia nodded and urged her horse in the direction of the stables.

"My valises and portmanteau are already packed. I'll be traveling to town with Lydia and you, Tommy," she said with gentle amusement. "I am sure Aunt Imogen will still expect you to accompany us to the ball."

"I have other plans," he said with a wink. "With a delightful widow who—"

"Tommy!" Sophia cried with a blush, knowing what the rogue had been about to say.

"Is that maidenly demureness I am detecting from a lady of five and twenty, one who fences, audaciously swims in the sea, rides astride in trousers and who I *know* kissed one Lord Sanderson last year in this very garden?"

She glared at him before laughing. Sophia had fallen lamentably short of expectation time and time again as she lived her life as if there were no promise of tomorrow.

"*When I grow old, I would like to swim in the sea,*" her thirteen-year-old sister Henrietta had said wistfully as she had stared at the crashing waves at the seaside town in Brighton one summer.

"*I daresay I would like to ride astride one day, in trousers!*" their mama had said with a chortle as they had named the adventures they would partake in if not for society's expectations and eventual censure, "*and even sell my paintings.*"

That had been said with an expression of desperate hunger. Her mother had a talent which few could aspire to, but Papa had thought it unladylike and vulgar to actually sell her work. What would people say? That phrase had been a common rebuke from his lips.

Sophia's father had looked on indulgently, with a smile on his face, and had shocked them all by saying, "*I would partake in a horse race with the best of them all. Mayhap a carriage race with the rakes and rogues of London!*"

"*And I would like to marry Lord Lyons,*" Sophia had boldly said to the utter shock of her parents, and the delight of her sister.

Sophia had distressed her aunt as she had endeavored to live her life freely, fulfill all the desires her family had held in their hearts, doing their adventures for them. As she accomplished each one, she would lie on the grass and stare at the heavens and whisper, "*Mama, Papa, Henrietta…. I did this…*" and spend a couple hours speaking to her departed family.

While she lived her life on the edge of society's censure, loneliness had crammed her heart full. The few times her aunt had tried to broach the topic of her finding a husband to marry she had shied away from the conversation. She had rejected the notion of ever forming such a lasting attachment. Marriage and a family were no longer in the cards for her. She had lost her family years ago, and Sophia could not bear the idea of letting anyone get that close again, to avoid repetition of such brutal loss and pain.

But she wanted to enjoy life to its fullest and all its offerings. Lately, she had been wondering about the pleasures of the flesh, she admitted with a guilty flush mounting her cheeks. And it had a lot to do with the passionate embrace in which she had caught Tommy with one of his lady loves at a country rout last year. A surge of longing had filled her heart and tears had pricked behind her lids as she'd watched them. Then she had turned away, wishing to give them some privacy.

Memories of being in William's arms had haunted her throughout that night, and when Lord Sanderson had whisked her onto the terrace and away from curious eyes, she had allowed him a kiss. Nothing had been roused in her breast, and with shock she had pulled away from the man. When William had kissed her, she had flamed in his embrace. Could it be that grief and pain had killed all desires in her heart and body?

Sophia urged her horse into a canter, truly wondering if she could continue the wildly improper avenues her musing had been merrily taking her. *An affair*. One of utter discretion before she put her most exciting plan into effect. She would depart from England's shores for Europe for another grand adventure. Or perhaps she should wait until she reached Versailles and then find herself a lover.

Utter madness, she chided herself, nudging her horse into a run toward the stables. The only thing she needed to concentrate on at the moment was ensuing her dear Lydia had a wonderful time in London, and to help her secure a proper match by the end of the Season.

Nothing more.

Once in the forecourt, she dismounted and handed over the horse to a stable lad, and quickly snuck inside. The butler, Mr. Ormsby, showed no reaction to her manner of dress. Sophia hurried down the long hallway, and then up the winding stairs when her aunt's voice halted her from below.

"Sophia?"

She closed her eyes briefly before turning around and peering down. "Yes, Aunt Imogen?"

Aunt Imogen held a vase of flowers—dahlias—in her hand. Her aunt's gaze skipped over the trousers, half-boots, and white shirt she wore. Disapproval furrowed her brows for a few seconds before she sighed.

"And whose outrageous dream are you acting out today?"

A lump formed in Sophia's throat and she wanted to rush down the stairs and fling herself into her aunt's embrace. Years ago, when a few of their neighbors had called her manners wild and improper, Sophia had explained tearily to her aunt that she wanted to live every dream her family had ever had but had been too afraid to explore. Her aunt had struggled to understand, but she too had missed her brother dreadfully, and had allowed Sophia her eccentricities. She had done her best to be discreet when warranted and had even offered to rent her own cottage with the inheritance of five hundred pounds from her father so as not to be a burden to her aunt's household with her more flamboyant ways. Her aunt had refused but had never shown such understanding before.

"It was Mama's own," she said, after taking a steady breath. "She…she had mentioned it once before when we were by the seaside, but in her diary…. she often spoke of being free to race across the moors, feeling the wind of her face as the horse thundered beneath her."

There was a contemplative air about her aunt as she considered Sophia.

"Well then, I am quite glad you experienced that, I do urge you to keep in mind that we have guests." Then she smiled and continued toward the drawing room.

With a smile, Sophia hurried to her room and stripped off the trousers and shirt. She stood in her knee-length drawers, corset and chemisette. She rang the bell for help with her corset and bounded breasts, but it was Lydia who arrived.

"Mama mentioned what she caught you in," Lydia said with a wide smile, ambling over to tug at the tight laces.

Sophia released a sigh of relief as the whale boned corset loosened and the bindings were removed. It had been tempting not to wear restrictive garments, but her breasts were too bountiful for her to be racing across the country without it. That would have been shocking and scandalous, and possibly even Tommy would have rebuked her behavior.

Lydia sat on the chaise longue by the window, a bright gleam in her expressive brown eyes. "I am terribly excited to be going to London tomorrow. This is my second Season, and I do hope it promises to be more fruitful than my first one! I've been missing for so long; I daresay all the *beaux* who'd been so promising are no longer on the marriage mart."

Lydia was three and twenty but was only entering her second Season due to a long bout of an infection of the lungs. Aunt Imogen had taken her to the country for fresh air and recovery a little over two years ago, and Lydia was quite keen on returning to town to reacquaint herself with the elegancies and frivolities of town life. Sophia had been her companion and friend for the last few years, and while she did not enjoy the offerings of the *ton*, she was quite happy to be there to support her friend.

"I'll try not to hover much as your chaperone," she said teasingly. "Perhaps you'll finally be able to get that kiss you have been dreaming of."

Lydia predictably blushed and tucked a strand of her vibrant red hair behind her ears. "Only if Lord Jeremy Prendergast is still unmarried! I did like him so very much when we met. But if not, I'll certainly not make a cake of myself and wear my heart on my sleeve. Another suitable lord will do for I am quite determined to secure a wonderful match by next month!"

Sophia tugged a light blue day dress from the

armoire and peeked around the dress at Lydia. "Within a month?"

"Yes," Lydia cried in mock horror. "I am three and twenty, a veritable spinster." Then she toed off her slippers and folded her feet onto the chaise. "Do you not wish to be married, Sophia? I cannot believe you do not hunger for a man of your own….and children…and best of all to be the mistress of your own home!"

I do not dream anymore.

But she dared not say it, hating to do anything to take that shine from Lydia's eyes.

"If someone suitable were to present himself, I might consider it," she said with a light laugh. *For an affair…nothing more.*

That excited Lydia, who jumped to her feet, grabbed Sophia's hand and tugged her to the bed. Sophia spent the next hour, laughing and making a list with Lydia on the kind of gentlemen who might be suitable.

No rakes. Not even the reformed ones.

He must be no older than two and thirty.

Must have a noteworthy title.

Sophia had rolled her eyes at that one, and Lydia had remarked nothing less than a viscount would do for her mother.

His kisses must be pleasant.

And at that…Sophia had shocked and titillated Lydia by saying, "If a kiss from your *beau* does not make your heart tremble and fire flames from your belly…. he will not do."

When Lydia had demanded more, Sophia had declined, but for the first time for some many years, that night she had dreamed again of William's kisses.

WANT TO KNOW WHAT HAPPENS NEXT?
CONTINUE READING…

FREE OFFER

SIGN UP TO MY NEWSLETTER TO CLAIM YOUR FREE BOOK!

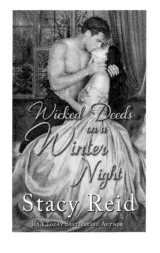

To claim your FREE copy of Wicked Deeds on a Winter Night, a delightful and sensual romp to indulge in your reading addiction, please click here.

Once you've signed up, you'll_be among the first to hear about my new releases, read excerpts you won't find anywhere else, and patriciate in subscriber's only giveaways and contest. I send out on dits once a month and on super special occasion I might send twice, and please know you can unsubscribe whenever we no longer zing.

Happy reading!
Stacy Reid

ACKNOWLEDGMENTS

I thank God every day for my family, friends, and writing. A special thank you to my husband. I love you so hard! You encourage me to dream and are always steadfast in your incredible support. You read all my drafts, offer such fantastic insight and encouragement. Thank you for designing my fabulous cover! Thank you for reminding me I am a warrior when I wanted to give up on so many things.

Thank you, Giselle Marks for being so wonderful and supportive always. You are a great critique partner and friend.

Readers, thank you for giving me a chance and reading my book! I hope you enjoyed and would consider leaving a review. Thank you!

ABOUT STACY

USA Today Bestselling author Stacy Reid writes sensual Historical and Paranormal Romances and is the published author of over twenty books. Her debut novella The Duke's Shotgun Wedding was a 2015 HOLT Award of Merit recipient in the Romance Novella category, and her bestselling Wedded by Scandal series is recommended as Top picks at Night Owl Reviews, Fresh Fiction Reviews, and The Romance Reviews.

Stacy lives a lot in the worlds she creates and actively speaks to her characters (aloud). She has a warrior way "Never give up on dreams!" When she's not writing, Stacy spends a copious amount of time binge-watching series like The Walking Dead, Altered Carbon, Rise of the Phoenixes, Ten Miles of Peach Blosson, and playing video games with her love. She also has a weakness for ice cream and will have it as her main course.

Stacy is represented by Jill Marsal at Marsal Lyon Literary Agency.

She is always happy to hear from readers and would love to connect with you via my Website, Facebook, and Twitter. To be the first to hear about her new releases, get cover reveals, and excerpts you won't find anywhere else, sign up for her newsletter, or join her over at Historical Hellions, her fan group!

Printed in Great Britain
by Amazon